SEALED

PROTECTION

Bone Frog Brotherhood Book 5

SHARON HAMILTON

SHARON HAMILTON'S BOOK LIST

SEAL BROTHERHOOD SERIES
Accidental SEAL (Book 1)
Fallen SEAL Legacy (Book 2)
SEAL Under Covers (Book 3)
SEAL The Deal (Book 4)
Cruisin' For A SEAL (Book 5)
SEAL My Destiny (Book 6)
SEAL Of My Heart (Book 7)
Fredo's Dream (Book 8)
SEAL My Love (Book 9)
SEAL Encounter (Book 1 Prequel)
SEAL Endeavor (Book 2 Prequel)
SEAL Brotherhood Box Set 1 (Accidental SEAL & Prequel)
SEAL Brotherhood Box Set 2 (Fallen SEAL & Prequel)
Ultimate SEAL Collection Vol. 1 (Books 1-4 + 2 Prequels)
Ultimate SEAL Collection Vol. 2 (Books 5-7)

BAD BOYS OF SEAL TEAM 3 SERIES
SEAL's Promise (Book 1)
SEAL My Home (Book 2)
SEAL's Code (Book 3)
Big Bad Boys Book (Books 1-3 of Bad Boys)

BAND OF BACHELORS SERIES
Lucas (Book 1)
Alex (Book 2)
Jake (Book 3)
Jake 2 (Book 4)
Big Band of Bachelors Bundle

TRUE BLUE SEALS SERIES
Zak (Includes prequel novella)

NASHVILLE SEAL SERIES
Nashville SEAL: Jameson (Books 1 & 2 combined)

SILVER SEALS
SEAL Love's Legacy

SLEEPER SEALS
Bachelor SEAL

STAND ALONE SEALS
SEAL's Goal: The Beautiful Game
Love Me Tender, Love You Hard

BONE FROG BROTHERHOOD SERIES
New Year's SEAL Dream (Book 1)
SEALed At The Altar (Book 2)
SEALed Forever (Book 3)
SEAL's Rescue (Book 4)
SEALed Protection (Book 5)

PARADISE SERIES
Paradise: In Search of Love

STANDALONE NOVELLAS
SEAL You In My Dreams (Magnolias and Moonshine)
SEAL Of Time (Trident Legacy)

FALL FROM GRACE SERIES (PARANORMAL)
Gideon: Heavenly Fall

GOLDEN VAMPIRES OF TUSCANY SERIES (PARANORMAL)
Honeymoon Bite (Book 1)
Mortal Bite (Book 2)
Christmas Bite (Book 3)
Midnight Bite (Book 4) Coming Fall 2019

THE GUARDIANS (PARANORMAL)
Heavenly Lover (Book 1)
Underworld Lover (Book 2)
Underworld Queen (Book 3)
Immortal Valentines A Paranormal Super Bundle

AUDIOBOOKS
Sharon Hamilton's books are available as audiobooks narrated
by J.D. Hart.

This is a work of fiction. Names, characters, places, brands, media, and incidents are either the product of the author's imagination or are used fictitiously. In many cases, liberties and intentional inaccuracies have been taken with rank, description of duties, locations and aspects of the SEAL community.

ABOUT THE BOOK

Navy SEAL Tucker Hudson has made all the right choices the second time around: a retread, re-joining SEAL Team 3 after ten years of wandering, he has a new wife, and now a new baby on the way. He struggles to hold on to his precious hard-won happiness, living a life he barely thought possible beside a woman who is in many ways stronger than he is.

Brandy has proven she has what it takes to be married to an elite warrior, including being left alone during his dangerous deployments. But as she welcomes their new addition, a dark cloud descends upon her family as evil shows up closer to home, making them all rethink their life plans.

Is it going to take more than their strong love for each other to protect everything they hold dear?

AUTHOR'S NOTE

I always dedicate my SEAL Brotherhood books to the brave men and women who defend our shores and keep us safe. Without their sacrifice, and that of their families—because a warrior's fight always includes his or her family—I wouldn't have the freedom and opportunity to make a living writing these stories. They sometimes pay the ultimate price so we can debate, argue, go have coffee with friends, raise our children and see them have children of their own.

One of my favorite tributes to warriors resides on many memorials, including one I saw honoring the fallen of WWII on an island in the Pacific:

"When you go home
Tell them of us, and say
For your tomorrow,
We gave our today."

These are my stories created out of my own imagination. Anything that is inaccurately portrayed is either my mistake, or done intentionally to disguise something I might have overheard over a beer or in the corner of one of the hangouts along the Coronado Strand.

I support two main charities. Navy SEAL/UDT Museum operates in Ft. Pierce, Florida. Please learn about this wonderful museum, all run by active and former SEALs and their friends and families, and who rely on public support, not that of the U.S. Government. www.navysealmuseum.org

IF YOU GOT ANY CLOSER, YOU WOULD HAVE TO ENLIST

I also support Wounded Warriors, who tirelessly bring together the warrior as well as the family members who are just learning to deal with their soldier's condition and have nowhere to turn. It is a long path to becoming well, but I've seen first-hand what this organization does for its warriors and the families who love them. Please give what your heart tells you is right. If you cannot give, volunteer at one of the many service centers all over the United States. Get involved. Do something meaningful for someone who gave so much of themselves, to families who have paid the price for your freedom. You'll find a family there unlike any other on the planet. www.woundedwarriorproject.org

CHAPTER 1

T UCKER HUDSON, DECORATED Navy SEAL from legendary SEAL Team 2, spent the entire weekend in San Diego hacking and pulling up old vines and shrubs that had lost their shape from plantings more than thirty years ago, as well as obliterating escaping bamboo invading from neighboring properties. He'd started with hand clippers, then moved on to large tree nips, electric hedge trimmers and finally a small chainsaw to remove the stubborn foliage. It was Brandy's vision that this area become a combination garden paradise and vegetable garden, even though it was technically the front yard of their new home.

If it was what Brandy wanted, Tucker was going to make it so, regardless of how sunburned and sweaty he got, or how much noise and dust he created. It was vegitative warfare this willing warrior was fighting for the bride of all his dreams, mother of his soon-to-b born son.

Well, that's what he was counting on—a son.

Of course, if Brandy wanted a girl, it would probably be a girl. He no longer marveled at how many of her dreams became reality. His job was to follow along the gilded path she created with her zest for life and her overall exuberance for living to the fullest.

She'd keep him young, with their over fifteen-year difference in age. When he was hobbling around on a cane, he'd still be her knight, fixing things and balancing himself on dangerous ladders to hang pictures or change light fixtures or drapes, just because Brandy wanted it that way.

Each time he stopped, gulping down half a quart of ice water, he'd glance over at the large boxes containing the gift palm trees they'd yet to plant in the ground. It was on his daily honey-do list, to water those plants, and every time he did so, he thought about the man who gifted them, Colin Riley – a man he met on his last mission.

As I've said before, I can't thank you enough for your wonderful gift of my daughter's life. These trees should reach the height of thirty feet or more, so I hope you will plant them where you can enjoy watching them grow, as you grow your family and enjoy your new home. But don't place them anywhere they will spoil that fantastic view.

I'm glad our paths have crossed. I hope someday to

be able to be more a part of your lives. While these trees grow, and hopefully before they get to be thirty feet, and I'm gone, I'd like to sit down and thank you in person and talk about a future that could be for all of us.

He'd memorized nearly every word, having read the card over so many times—something he never would admit to Brandy. He noted the many-fingered branches fluttered in the breeze as if saying hello. If he put those roots in Brandy's Secret Garden, they'd grow. That would mean the man who'd sent them would become more and more a fixture in their lives.

He hadn't decided whether or not that was a good thing.

TUCKER KNEW HIS next deployment was coming up in another thirty days. He'd promised Brandy that he'd be home for the baby's birth, and he hoped he could keep that vow. But the short trip back to the Canary Islands required his leadership, since their normal team leader, Chief Kyle Lansdowne, was off on special assignment to the State Department. Although technically still a newer member of the squad, he'd done ten years previous before his re-enlistment and re-qualification. At forty-one years of age, he was one of the oldest members. Outranked by nearly everyone, the guys still looked upon him as the unofficial LPO in Kyle' absence. And that's why Kyle wanted him on mission.

The job would revisit some of the bad guys they'd encountered several months ago, when they rescued the daughter of the man who gave him the potted palm trees.

He'd tried to get billionaire Colin Riley's face and the squeak of his wheelchair out of his mind, but the man was a stubborn memory. He knew why. Riley had scratched an itch that was now inflamed. He'd dared to offer Tucker a job lining up a secret security force for good. But that would mean that Riley would *own* Tucker. He wasn't going to even let the man give him a proper presentation. The answer was no before Riley could finish his first imaginary PowerPoint.

No one, not even a billionaire offering a lifestyle he could only fantasize about, was ever going to own Tucker Hudson. He hadn't become a SEAL for fame or fortune. He wasn't about to change that all now.

But on days like these, when he was working in the yard and trying to get the house into shape to prepare for the new baby, it would have been nice to rent some equipment to make it a little easier on his body. Unlike Colin Riley, Tucker and Brandy's funds were precarious. They were living on one salary, and even as a SEAL, the pay wasn't great.

They'd just bought a major fixer on the island, rgrown, neglected and mercifully hidden from the other large homes in the neighborhood. Their furniture came from second-hand stores. The new refrigerator they bought had a six-inch dent in the door and was missing handles. The new stove had a cracked black glass door. These were all things that could be fixed, of course, but after they finished purchasing the new vanity and toilet for their bathroom. Everything they bought came from some Asian warehouse where not a word of English was spoken. The damned place smelled of fish, reminding him of some of the villages in Africa and South America. All the cabinets, appliances, and fixtures were cosmetically damaged but deeply discounted.

It was a delicate balance, calculating where their next paycheck would be spent. With luck, it would all be complete before the new arrival.

He was expecting some help from his childhood best friend, Brawley Hanks, as well as T.J. Talbot and several other guys from Team 3. Brandy was off getting things for a "thank you" barbeque after a few hours of work and drinking beers until the stars came out. He'd made a firepit, lined it with bricks, and found an old grate he could use as a spark catcher. He wanted to have a bonfire without setting the neighbors' houses on fire.

But damn, he heard that mechanical whine fro Riley's wheelchair again and wished he could wipe memory, because now it was becoming really annoying. He turned up the music on his second-hand paint-spattered boombox, which successfully masked the noise by blaring country music from a local AM station.

He dug out several deep roots of shrubs he'd castrated and tossed them to the side. He skimmed the top hardpan layer with a shovel and discovered a soft sandy soil underneath that could eventually be habitable for Brandy's garden.

His whole life had changed dramatically after that fateful New Years' eve, two and a half years ago—the night of Brawley and Dorie's wedding, where he watched Brandy walk down the aisle behind the other bridesmaids.

He never was able to recover from that vision of her and that damned bustier, which accentuated the features he loved most in women: their bosoms and curvy hips.

That brought a smile to his face. They'd both been running away from something that night, he remembered. He was running away from loneliness, not on a Team at that time but desperately needing the connection. Brandy was running away from the same thing but was the only one being honest with herself. She wanted one perfect night. Well, hell, he happened to be here and available, and the attraction was instantaneous, even when he had to hold her hair back as she threw up. She was dosing. Tucker was just fishing. And like two shooting stars in the night sky, they slammed into one another. And that was it.

It was a simple case of undeniable chemistry. Not a damned thing he could do about it, either. Not that he wanted to.

Now he was going to have a little "orbit" of his own. That's what he and Brawley had called children when they were growing up. Little annoying things who got in the way. Except now he had a whole new appreciation for offspring. He'd been given a miracle, even though he was a poor, dumb frogman. He wondered why God had trusted him to become a father. But he had a fierce love for Brandy that loomed larger than a battleship. And that gave him hope for a bright future.

Although he would never tell a soul this, he believed in the healing power of true love. He was a big, tough SEAL, but he was a hopeless romantic.

Brandy drove up in the Hummer, following the driveway on the right side of the property. She stopped close to where he was standing, and he threw his shovel down to help her get out of the truck. Before he could get there, she'd slid out until her dangling feet touched the ground. Her belly must have been infringing on h lungs, because just as he arrived at her side, she pa closed her eyes, and took several slow, deep breaths.

"I could have helped you. Next time, don't be so impatient, Brandy."

She gave him a sweet smile, her cheeks pink and plump, like the rest of her.

"Oh, stop it, Tucker, I'm not an invalid."

"But I want to help you, sweetheart."

She patted her palm against his cheek. "Silly man. Women have been having babies for thousands of years and managed quite well."

He wrapped his arms around her and forced her to hug him back, as he whispered in her ear, "But they don't drive Hummers that they have to HALO jump from. Don't do that anymore, okay, sweetheart?"

Brandy's VW bug was in the shop until Monday. But she'd not been able to drive it the past couple of weeks because she couldn't fit behind the steering wheel. He didn't have to mention that at all.

She relaxed and squeezed him back. "My protector."

"Always." He meant it.

He rounded the truck, retrieving the two grocery bags, and then walked beside her into the house.

"Where's your help?" she asked.

"Delayed." He set the bags on the countertop and ⸺rted through the contents. Finding two five-pound ⸺ages of marked down hamburger meat, he quickly placed it in the refrigerator then examined her other purchases. He was delighted to find a half gallon of rocky road ice cream. "Nice!" He held the package up to her smiling face.

"Not sure if we have any more of that chocolate syrup, but I bought whipped cream."

He shook the metal can and wiggled his eyebrows. "Dangerous!"

"Uh-huh. I think that's where the chocolate syrup went." She blushed, grabbed the whipped cream, and slipped it next to the hamburger meat. Tucker put the ice cream in the freezer.

She handed him three six-packs of beer bottles, one at a time. Then she handed him a large pre-made salad with dressing and a dozen ears of corn.

"If everyone comes, we'll have to split the corn in half. And I got some fresh cherry tomatoes, but I'd like to go to the Farmer's Market tomorrow, if you're game to get more veggies."

"Sure thing. Let's go early."

"I miss not being able to run over to Dad's store and just pick stuff up."

Tucker wrapped his arm around Brandy's non-existent waist. "But now he's free to travel, and he's happy, babe. Jillian's taking good care of him."

"Not complaining," she sighed as she leaned i- him, placing the side of her face against his che can't wait to *not* be pregnant. I want to see her little face. I'd also like to be able to see my toes again, take a bath, put my own shoes on—stuff like that."

Tucker snickered softly but didn't correct her. He accepted the fact that she was probably right—they'd be having a daughter. How women knew these things mystified him.

"Hello?" Brawley's booming voice nearly vibrated the windows.

Tucker walked into the living room and found his best friend carrying a large brown shopping bag. "What did you bring?"

"Some energy drinks, beer, water, more beer, and a pie."

Tucker noticed Brawley's skin was tanned, his eyes were clear, and he appeared to be in about the best shape of his life. These days, he no longer smelled of alcohol, either. He'd spent several months in a private brain clinic while he slowly came back to the living, becoming more and more the man Tucker used to know. He'd just transitioned to work support for the Teams as a BUD/S instructor until he could get his twenty in. Alcohol wasn't restricted but closely monitored. Tucker could see he was following the program.

"You look like you've been enjoying the beach," d Tucker.

"Only this time I'm *watching* the wet and sandy.

Were we ever that dumb, Tucker? Those little tadpoles don't know shit about anything. They look like they've just begun to shave."

"I think we were the same," Tucker disagreed.

"Nope. You never looked like a boy. You were built like a man from the first time I hurled that pitch at you and you hit it over the fence. My coach said we were going to have to check your birth certificate. All that black hair all over your body when you were ten. Fuckin' ten, damn you!"

Tucker ducked so Brawley's punch didn't connect. "Dorie coming later on?"

"Yup, I'm supposed to text her when you're ready." He leaned around Tucker to speak to his wife. "Brandy? She's sorry she couldn't get a sitter to come help you today."

Brawley and his wife had four-month-old twin boys. They also had a three-year-old daughter, Jessica.

"No worries. We're doing very simple tonight. Hamburgers, homemade potato salad, green salad, and corn. I got ice cream for dessert. Just easy stuff. No candlelight gourmet meals tonight," she answered. "But we'll have plenty, so I hope she'll come and bring the kids."

Several minutes later, three other Team Guys arrived, each bringing more beer and a couple mor salads. Fredo brought a rototiller and more gar tools in the back of his beater truck, including a flat scraper Tucker grabbed onto right away for stubbing out the tufts and roots in the future garden area. He also brought some scrap lumber for the firepit.

It was a typical SEAL work party. There was lots of attitude, some practical joking that had them chasing after each other, dousing themselves with water bottles or beer, and long silent minutes of solid work. Tucker laid out what had to be done, and without assigning anyone to any specific task, the men just filled in, working as one cohesive team.

That's how they worked overseas too. It was like they maintained a hive brain. One person's good idea would be supported and acted upon by others. It didn't take long before the entire front yard area was tilled, raked, and looked like powdered chocolate, instead of the abandoned weed fest it was when they first bought the home.

T.J. began to build a berm running parallel to the sidewalk, extending it along the side of the driveway. The rest of the men joined in, until it was complete.

"You gonna put in a fence on top? asked Fredo.

Tucker thought that was an excellent idea. "Maybe just a couple of feet high, tall enough to keep a toddler from escaping, yes! Gonna have to get the materials next paycheck, though."

"You got some extras left over from your new

fence, T.J." Fredo nodded to the tall medic.

"I'll get Joe Benson. You remember? Frankie's dad? We'll come over and build that for you," said T.J.

"Dude, now you're making me feel obligated. Spoiling me." Tucker was a little embarrassed.

"Just say thank you, Tuck. I don't think you fully comprehend what it's going to be like here very soon. Life will never be the same," T.J. returned.

Fredo stepped up and pat his shoulder. The Mexican SEAL was more than a foot shorter. "We're helping you out now, 'cause no way you'll see us hanging around after the baby comes. I'll let Mia and the wives do all that shit."

Fredo's comments drew much agreement.

The men stacked Tucker's tools beside the front porch and returned the other tools and equipment to the bed of Fredo's truck. Tucker could hear soft music coming from the warm, orange insides of their little fixer as Brandy was beginning to set things out on two long folding tables. She brought a tray of hamburgers ready for the grill and turned the gas on to warm it up.

Her voice caught all of their attention. "You guys go on inside and wash up. You can text the girls to come over. I wanted to eat in about thirty minutes. That sound fine?"

"Yes, ma'am," was the resounding response.

As two of the men went inside, looking down

their cells, T.J. and Tucker moved several stumps next to the firepit, adding them to the large boulders to create makeshift stools for later enjoyment. An old wine half barrel was rolled over to the join the circle.

T.J. dusted his hands together and wiped his forehead with the back of his shirt sleeve. He pointed to the palm trees, standing to attention, their long green fingers waving. "Those are real cool, Tucker. Where are you going to put these?"

"Haven't decided."

"I'd put them side by side up front along the berm. Sort of makes a statement, you know?"

Tucker examined the area where the berm turned to follow along the driveway. If he got a few more, he could make a palm tree entrance that would befit the Queen of Sheba.

He shook the vision off and nodded in the direction of the front. "I like putting them up front."

It would be the furthest from the house possible. But they'd be planted. And maybe they'd guard his little family like lions on a grand, gated entrance.

CHAPTER 2

BRANDY WAS RELEGATED to their large second-hand recliner and made to prop her feet up. Fredo's wife, Mia, had noticed her ankles were swollen from the heat and from being on them most the day. Dorie sat next to her with the twins fast asleep in a double stroller. Luci and Mia were cleaning up dishes in the kitchen and putting away leftovers.

Dorie's daughter, Jessica, had been running wild outside with several of the other kids, including Fredo and Mia's Ricardo and their twin toddlers. Danny and Luci Begay's two boys—Griffin and his adopted Iraqi boy, Ali—had been conducting sniper attacks on the adult population, and occasionally the other children.

At home, Griffin was Ali's favorite target. Here, the boys used cherry tomatoes plucked from Brandy's green salad. Every one of the children had red stains on their clothes and on their faces. Most of the SEALs did as well.

As Ali ran past Brandy, she grabbed him by the arm and firmly stopped his forward march.

"Ali, not inside the house!" She kept her grip on his upper arm until she saw a forlorn nod after several seconds of trying to wiggle free. She pulled him toward her. "I mean it, Ali. You're going to get one of the other ones hurt. They're smaller and can't keep up. And I've just painted the inside of this house, unless you want to come and spend all day repainting it. Right?"

His dark eyes grimaced as the group of younger children accordioned behind him, finally catching up. The little orphan was embarrassed, she could tell. Her heart softened.

She scanned the crowd of children and knew these were little eyes of future SEALs. At this age, Tucker would have been right in the middle of them.

Dorie inserted herself into the conversation. "Griffin, you know better. You have to show your brother. Don't let him get into trouble."

Griffin spouted off, "But he started it. It was all his idea. I told him!"

That caught the attention of Luci Begay from the kitchen. "You two!" she shouted, wiping her hands on a towel. "What am I going to do with you? Give me that," she demanded of Ali.

He pulled away defiantly, clutching the slingshot Danny had made for him out of an old inner tube and remnants of their burned-out soccer stadium.

"I won't do it inside. I promise. Honest." His expression was pure angel, and Brandy could see all the stories were true. He was so advanced for his age in physical ability, and, because of how he'd had to live in the war zone, he was stronger and faster than anyone else. He'd seen things none of the other children ever would, if they were lucky. Now in second grade, he was prone to getting into fights with much older boys.

And he usually won.

Luci sighed and told them to go outside and pick on the men sitting around the firepit. "And be careful that Jessica, Courtney, and the twins don't get hurt."

Ali and Griffin instantly showed expressions of horror. To make matters worse, Courtney Talbot scolded them in her pert, five-year-old voice. "Your mother's right. Don't you know you have to be nice to girls?" She gave the hands-on-her-hips pose just like a little mother.

In the background, Ricardo snickered, and Ali whirled around to face him but thought better of it before he could begin his defensive attack.

"What's this?" said Brawley, who suddenly appeared from the outside, holding Jessica.

"I started it," giggled Brandy. "This is a no tomato zone." She pointed to Ali's slingshot and his sticky red fingers.

"Oh, I get it now," Brawley said with a grin. He kneeled next to Brandy and motioned for the group to come closer as he set down the squirming Jessica. In hushed voice, he began creating a conspiracy the children were all too eager to participate in. "Let's plan a sneak attack on the insurgents out there. Not much fun attacking babies and mothers, is it?"

The children shook their heads in unison.

"Besides, they have ways of ruining your equipment." He was pointing to Ali's slingshot, but all four wives burst out laughing. Brawley himself was having difficulty keeping a straight face and kept his focus on the serious faces of his co-conspirators.

"You need more ammunition?" Brandy asked.

"Yes, ma'am. You got any?"

"There's another basket in the refrigerator. I guess this is for a good cause, but Brawley Hanks, if just one of those tomatoes lands anywhere in my house, you're gonna personally re-paint the whole place, inside and out!"

Brawley turned to the kids again after retrieving the red orbs from the refrigerator. "You see what I mean? You don't piss off the wife of a SEAL."

He winked at Dorie who beamed back at him. Brandy saw the love between them in full bloom again. It warmed her soul to see this. She hoped their hard ys were finally behind them.

Brawley left with his merry band of outlaws in tow. They tiptoed out the kitchen door. Within seconds, their little bodies could be seen rounding the outside of the house, Brawley crouching in the lead. Jessica wandered back in, lethargic, seeking her mother's lap, rubbing her eyes.

Five minutes later, Brandy heard the pirate attack coming from the front yard with screams and shouts of tomato warfare piercing the peaceful night air.

SHE STOOD IN the doorway while Tucker helped their guests coral all the kids and see everyone safely off. He ran down the driveway toward her, barefoot, in his faded and ragged jeans, shirtless and happy, and it took her breath away. At forty-one years of age, he'd kept his massive shoulders and corded arms, and slim waist (at least compared to his upper torso) without an ounce of extra fat anywhere. He easily could have played professional football; he was so magnificently put together. She felt like the luckiest woman in the world.

As he approached, her hands went to her lower belly, rubbing their baby as she slept.

"Look at you, sweetheart! All ripe and ready to burst!" he whispered before he kissed her.

"Now I know why I feel so big," she answered, continuing to rub. Tucker's hand joined hers in the gentle baby massage.

"You *are* pretty big. Are you sure we got the dates right? You look ready to go, no more of this three-to-four-week stuff," he said.

"I was just wondering that until I watched your body move down the driveway like some huge, Greek god. Tucker, the baby is big, because of—well, look at *you*!"

"So what you're sayin' is that I'm going to have an Amazon daughter?" He cocked his head as if bracing for a slap.

"At least I'll be there to school her in the advantages of being a big girl. That way, perhaps she won't have to go through all the same things I did."

Tucker looked down at his toes. He was thinking about something, and Brandy could tell he was hesitant to speak it out loud.

"Go on. Spill it." She threw her arms around his neck, bellied up to him so he could feel the baby kicking, and said, "Whatever it is, I want to hear it."

He tenderly stroked her cheek with the back of his fingers then sifted through her hair, ending up with a long forefinger rubbing across her lips. "I think it was harder on you because you lost your mom just when a girl probably needs her mom the most. Does that make sense?"

"You were a woman in your past life, or is there

something you're needing to tell me?" She was stifling a smile, but it was tough.

"Nah, I don't understand women much at all. But I know you, Brandy. And I know what's in your heart, I think. I think that's why you'll be a great mom, boy or girl. Because you know how it feels to not have one while you're still young, sweetheart. And you're going to make up for whatever you didn't get."

She was stunned. She'd never thought about it that way. The constant refrain of "Dad is the best dad a girl could ever want, and he's done the perfect job," was the only thing she allowed herself to consider. But viewing it now, Tucker was right.

"Did I mess up?" he asked, tipping back her chin with his thumb and two fingers. His eyebrows rose in a question.

"Not at all. You're more perceptive than I ever thought a man could be. You do know me. You know everything about me. And what I haven't told you, you've just learned on your own. I thought women were the only ones who were supposed to do that."

He leaned back on his heels, separating their chests as he arched backward. "Ah, well, I think it's because I never met anyone quite like you. I never had this. And I'm not letting it go. Like you said, it was the perfect start. I'm up for keeping it that way, aren't you?"

"Absolutely, Tucker. We've both waited a long time

to have our hearts fed the way they are now. I'm ready to spread the love to our baby."

She followed him to the fire pit, the embers glowing red but without flame. He brushed aside the coals and covered them with dirt then replaced the grate and stood with her, examining the stars above. A gentle breeze blew off the ocean, and the salty air was soothing. She knew she'd sleep better tonight. They'd both worked hard today and enjoyed sharing their project with their extended family.

The wind kicked up with more intensity, rustling the foliage at the neighbor's property line. It also caused the palm trees, still in their square wooden pots, to flutter, sounding more like a gentle waterfall.

He was turning to go inside, but she stopped him.

"Can we plant these tomorrow?" she asked, pointing to their gift.

"Okay. T.J. gave me a good idea today about putting them at the front of the property, like sentries."

"Sentries? I don't get it."

"Like two big guards at a gate. Like big lions on a gate."

"Guarding our fortress kind of thing?" She was still puzzled.

"Well, yes, and no. A statement of strength and grandeur, I think he meant. And power. Like they'll ward off evil spirits. Protect our family."

She shuddered. It never was a pleasant thought considering all the danger there was out there in the real world. Her warm and satisfying world was a bubble she never wanted to burst.

"It's a good thing, Brandy. That way, we can see these trees, as they grow, silhouetted against the orange sky, like it does here at sundown nearly every night. We'll see those trees, and we'll feel how strong our love is. How nothing can hurt us ever."

"Okay. Well, they don't look very majestic right now. Kind of stumpy but with lots of promise. Someday, like the man said, they'll be thirty feet or more." She was still slightly alarmed with where the conversation was going. "Are you thinking this way because of who gave them to us?"

"Maybe." He shrugged. "I don't know, probably a stupid thought." He chuckled before he continued. "It sounded better when T.J. said it, that's all."

She laughed at his return to being light-hearted.

"I think that sounds like a great idea, Tucker. We're creating a dynasty here. It's the start of a new adventure."

He wrapped his arm around her shoulder, and they headed to the door. Just before she stepped over the ledge, something made her turn and glance over her shoulder at the palm trees fluttering in the shadows. They were nearly invisible. She leaned back to stu the sprinkling of stardust one more time before she said good night to the *outside* world.

She was going to dream tonight with great anticipation—all about her *inside* world and the young life waiting to be born.

CHAPTER 3

TUCKER GOT HIS orders two weeks later. The mission had been delayed another thirty days, which came as a great relief to him, since it meant he would not miss the birth of their child. But the bad news was that the deployment was indeterminate, which meant it might be longer than previously expected.

Their previous mission to the Canaries had been considered a fluke. They'd followed the trail of the missing American aid worker, Jenna Riley, who had been kidnapped and sold to the Dutch billionaire Jens VanValle in Nigeria and pirated away to his compound on Gran Canaria Island. In the firefight, the Dutchie was killed. Tucker didn't want to go anywhere near that place again and considered it a stroke of extremely good luck they'd made it out of there without Team casualties or sparking an international incident.

He was disappointed when he read that they'd be

going back to the same island, this time to capture several kingpins the State Department had identified as being leaders of the organization in Nigeria. He knew human trafficking was spreading all over the world, but he was surprised it had spread to a mainly tourist location where the local police and militia would do just about anything to keep things quiet so as not to interfere with their primary industry.

He had lots of questions about going there. He also wondered about Colin Riley's involvement in this mission, since Riley practically bankrolled the last one. Their mission partner, a former FSK officer-turned aid worker, Sven Tolar, told him that the home of the trafficking cell was located near the Nigerian capital and operated with the full cooperation and protection of the local government. So why the Canaries?

He'd ask his questions when they called the Team meeting, which would be very soon. He'd been given a list of shots to make sure he was up-to-date on, and the usual reminder about getting his affairs in order, which pissed him off every time.

But he'd be home for the baby, and right now, that was where he was laser focused. He and T.J. scheduled the workday with Shannon's former father-in-law, so they could build that small fence and get the palm trees planted like he'd promised.

He hoped Brandy wouldn't go into labor before

then.

Brandy seemed to perk up after the party. She turned the upstairs into a projects room where she set up her sewing workshop. He'd laid out sawhorses with full sheets of plywood on top, so she had room to cut and lay out curtains she was making, as well as a patchwork bedspread and other things for the baby's room. The Team wives bought them a new crib, and a beautiful rocking chair to match. These were the only pieces of furniture that weren't purchased at the second-hand furniture store or on eBay.

She was feeling so good that he brought her to the home improvement store to shop for the final things they needed in the bathroom.

"Now, remember, we can't buy the top of the line. Just enough to get by for now. We can always replace fixtures later on as we get more settled, okay?" he'd warned her.

"Gotcha. But, Tucker, I would like to see if we can find something that would fit on that refrigerator door. I'm breaking my nails trying to get it open all the time."

"We'll see. Might have to get that handle made. Those things change from year to year, and since it was a closeout, don't get your hopes up."

He could see she was going to object, so he interrupted her.

"We'll try, sweetheart. I promise."

That left her with a smile on her face.

They ran into another Team Guy and his wife from Team 5, Bryce and Geraldine Tanner. Tucker had served with Tanner during his first enlistment. The couple was around his own age and now had four kids in tow, all girls. The two older teenagers were fixated on their cell phones and didn't look up during introductions. Their father yanked the phones from their fingers and put them in his shirt pocket.

"There you go," said Bryce. "Problem solved." He gave a wide, confident smile.

"Daddy!" the taller one stomped and crossed her arms. She appeared to try to perse her lips, but her pink braces got in the way. Her fingernails were painted ten different colors.

Geraldine shook her head and nodded to Brandy's belly. "Kids. Hope you have boys. They're easier, I've been told!" she sighed.

Tucker noticed Brandy was eyeing the teens closely. Then she spoke up.

"Do you guys live on Coronado?"

"We sure do. But we're busting out at the seams, so we might be moving. You guys bought a neat place, I hear," answered Geraldine. "And call me Geri. That was nice of you, Tucker, but now I feel like I'm being scolded by my grandmother."

"Geri, then. How old are your girls?" Brandy asked.

"Fourteen and fifteen, going on thirty," answered Bryce.

"So they don't drive, then?"

"No. Are you asking if they babysit?" Geri asked.

"Well, I was thinking. I probably won't need anyone for a few months at least, but when the baby's maybe four months, yes, perhaps."

Geri leaned over, closer to Brandy, and whispered, "Most of us do trades. That way we don't have to pay for sitters, if you know what I mean. But they'd be delighted, I'm sure. Right, girls?"

"We'd love to," the shorter one said.

The older girl was still scowling from her father's confiscation.

Tucker put his arm around Brandy's waist. "We'll have to stoke up the BBQ and have you guys over."

"From the looks of things, perhaps you should let us do the honors," Bryce said.

Everyone laughed.

"I always hate to descend on someone else's home with our big family," said Geri. "Much easier for us to entertain you. Let's do it soon, if you can."

"Fair enough. Give me a call when you have a free evening," Tucker chuckled.

"GOOD THINKING," TUCKER said to his wife while they

were walking away. "But don't you think they're kind of young?"

"Oh, I'd have them do it together. But just for your information, I started getting paid to babysit at twelve, or even a little younger. Not for late nights, of course, but I was in high demand."

"I'll just bet you were," he chuckled. "We'll talk to them a little more, and if you feel comfortable, I'll go along with it. Of course, your dad and Jillian will be jealous as hell. Don't forget that."

"I know. I'm just planning ahead."

That stopped him in his tracks. Brandy walked ahead several steps, pushing their cart, until she realized he had stayed behind. She turned and cocked her head. "Tucker?"

He slowly approached, reached out to hold her face in his palms, and kissed her. "And just how many children were you planning on having, my dear? Or were you never going to tell me?"

Brandy blushed. But he loved that look that said her secret had been outed. She struggled to get away, but he held her close.

"Tell me, Brandy—"

"You never know, do you?" Her blush was still prominent, her chest blotchy red. She avoided eye contact, even though he was kissing her. They were blocking an aisle, but Tucker was driven.

"Two? Three? Four? More?" he called off to her between kisses, as softly as he could.

"Don't be silly. Let's start with one and see how that goes. And, Tucker, you're stopping traffic." She waived her arms, pointing behind him, so he let her go.

Brandy smoothed her hair, straightened her top, and let out a big sigh. She continued ahead of him again.

She was a miracle, this lovely woman who had agreed to be his wife. Had anyone else kept that kind of a secret from him, he'd have found it totally unattractive. But Brandy's schemes were like chocolate syrup and whipped cream. He was totally turned on by the fact that she wanted more babies.

And he'd love giving them to her.

CHAPTER 4

STEVEN COOK AND his new wife, Jillian, offered to take them out to dinner. The timing of her dad's offer was great. Brandy began to feel tired the week after the party. She'd completed the room decorations, finished the quilt, and got it ready to be sent out to the topper to finish it off. None of her clothes seemed to fit right and she was finding it hard to sleep. She knew time was getting very close.

So the offer of a nice dinner that meant she didn't have to cook was pure luxury.

Jillian and her father were so much in love. Brandy was glad that it was something she and Tucker shared. Otherwise, it would have been unbearable to be with them. She didn't have to use too much imagination to understand why Jillian occasionally jumped and giggled nervously. Tucker had sometimes made little secret sexual advances to Brandy under the table in front of their friends as well. But it was not something she expected her *father* to do.

She knew Jillian was a little uncomfortable with such a public display of affection, so Brandy interrupted the conversation about gardens and gardening to lean forward and scold her father and her new stepmother.

"Dad? Jillian? I get it. But you're getting a little over the top. If you want to fool around, let's all leave so you can do that. But you don't have to show me how much you'd rather be doing something else than sitting here talking to Tucker and me."

Now she'd done it. She wished she could take back her words. No one was making a move, and her father and Jillian's mouths had dropped open. Tucker was squirming in his seat, tapping his foot against hers under the table, but his hands were safely folded on the tabletop.

Overwhelmed, all of a sudden, Brandy burst out in tears. Her sobs were long. Hot, gushing tears ran down her cheeks, her neck, and into the top of her blouse. Then a strange sensation began in her upper chest. She looked down, placed her palm against her right breast and saw there was moisture there. She was shocked, which temporarily slowed her heaving chest.

Jillian took quick notice, taking her other hand in hers. "It's all right, sweetie. That's normal. You're beginning to lactate. Perfectly natural."

SEALED PROTECTION

Brandy didn't want to be talking to Jillian right now about her pregnancy. She wanted it to be her mother she was talking to. Her heart broke as she remembered her mother would never see her child, would not be there for her in the delivery room. She didn't want to take lactating advice from the woman her father was fondling and showing off like a high schooler. It was all wrong.

The tears burst forth again. She couldn't speak. It was like her eyes and her lungs were connected by something other than her brain, and it didn't have anything to do with her mouth, either. Her emotions rose to near panic levels. The sobbing resumed, and when Tucker put his arm around her, whispering something in her ear, she jumped at his touch. She knew it upset him because he tried to stifle his jump in reflex.

"Brandy, are you all right?" her father asked her.

It felt like he was clear across the room and his voice was muffled. For just a second, she couldn't recognize his face or remember his name. And then the wave of emotions washed over her again and she inhaled deep and let out a muffled scream.

Something warm and wet was happening between her legs. Her first thought was embarrassment, that she'd lost feeling and wet her pants. But as she concentrated on it, she discovered it had nothing to do with her bladder.

Tucker still had his arm around her. "What is it, Brandy?"

"My water's broken."

They cancelled dinner. Her father wanted to come with them to the hospital, but Brandy wouldn't have it. She knew it would make her more nervous. Tucker was the only one who could keep her calm and help her do this. After all the days she'd wondered how it would go, her new adventure had finally started.

Tucker called ahead, and the hospital staff was ready for her when they arrived. She was beginning to have sharp pains first in her lower back area then rolling up the sides of her stomach. The juncture between her legs was pulsing, and she could feel every muscle. As they were wheeling her up to the exam room, the baby kicked and nearly knocked her breath out.

"Wow, she's not happy, Tucker. She just kicked me."

"Not a thing to worry about. Glad she's strong. She's just letting you know she's damn good and ready. That's a good thing, sweetheart."

He had insisted on driving her wheelchair even though it was not hospital policy for him to do so. The admitting nurse jumped back nearly a foot after he glared back at her when she told him she'd take the chair.

By the time they got upstairs, she was already beginning to have small contractions. Tucker asked for some water, and the nurse quickly produced a small cup for her to take. The cool liquid tasted delicious. Their doctor hadn't arrived yet, so temporarily they admitted her to a room after the delivery nurse confirmed her water had broken, and she was in fact beginning to have contractions. They helped her change into a gown, and a monitor was placed on her belly.

Tucker stood idly by, his face long, as he watched everything the two nurses did. He made a couple of suggestions and a correction to the head nurse until he was ordered out of the room.

He refused.

"Come here and hold my hand, but you gotta let them do what they know how to do, Tucker. You need to trust them, or you'll start making me nervous too."

Tucker was by her side, squeezing her hand, just as a big contraction overtook her body, waking her up to the fact that she was indeed going to feel some major pain.

"They were right. Everyone was right!" she said announced to the whole floor.

"Right about what, hon?" the nurse whispered calmly.

"It hurts. It's gonna hurt."

The older woman smiled. "Now, sir, you have a job. You're here to help her with the pain. Distract her and the time will go by much quicker. You're her coach, but you're also her support."

SIX HOURS LATER, Kimberly Lynne Hudson came into the world weighing just an ounce over nine pounds. She didn't seem to mind that her father cut the cord that had her tethered to her mom. Her first cries were robust, her arms and legs moved powerfully, objecting to the bright lights and the fact that the she was in a room with all kinds of new noises and strange people. Her body was covered in dark hair, even her chest and legs, just like her father. She was cleaned, weighed, and wrapped tightly in a blanket, and given back to her mother.

Earlier, when Tucker had been given the scissors to tie the cord, he just stood there, having to be prodded at first. But as Kimberly was brought back to Brandy's side, he shook off the shock of what had just happened, and Brandy saw tears well up and then spill over his cheeks, dripping onto his light blue hospital gown.

The baby looked up at Brandy, blinking, trying to focus as she cooed and whispered back to her. "We're so happy you're here. What a beautiful baby you are, Kimberly. Look, this is daddy," she said as she angled the baby to face Tucker.

"See that big guy? He's not really as scary as he looks. He's your father, and he loves you."

She heard Tucker mumble, "I do. Er—he does!"

He lowered his face to give the baby a kiss on her forehead, and Brandy touched his cheek. "We did good, Tucker."

"It's a miracle, Brandy. I love her so much already. Thank you, sweetheart." He kissed her while she continued to stroke his cheek.

The baby took her first feeding ravenously.

"You little vampire," Tucker whispered to her.

"Shush. That's not nice. She's worked hard, and now she needs some sustenance."

When the baby fell asleep, she handed her to Tucker who sat in the corner of the dimly lit room while Brandy dozed off.

At last, they were a family.

The beginning of our dynasty.

CHAPTER 5

O F COURSE, THE mandatory pre-deployment Team meeting was called for the day Tucker brought Brandy and Kimberly home from the hospital. He'd spent the night before with them, resting off and on in the large armed chair in the corner of her hospital room. He held Kimberly to give Brandy frequent breaks so she could rest. Several times, the nurses tried to take the baby away when he'd fallen asleep, yet he refused to relinquish his prize. It was what the two of them had discussed prior to her admission. They both wanted as much time holding their daughter as they could.

Only once, he begrudgingly let the nurse take Kimberly away for an early morning clean up and vitals check. Brandy's doctor, who sported some serious tats on his muscled forearms, cleared them for the return home that morning. Tucker pegged him as a former Team Guy.

Just after the doctor left, Tucker broke the news to his wife.

"I'm so sorry, sweetheart. The worst timing." Tucker knew she understood, but still felt horrible about it. "It shouldn't be a long meeting, couple of hours at most."

The hospital refused to delay their departure, so he planned on taking her home and then heading back to base for the meeting.

"I'm good. If I need anything, I'll text you. Maybe you could call Dad before we go? They haven't seen the baby. Might be a nice time for them to come over."

"Good idea. I should have thought of that." He smacked his forehead with his palm.

Brandy giggled. "I think you're a little sleep deprived. You be careful on the road today, Tucker."

He returned a smirk. "There you go, still worrying about me. You're the one who needs tending to. I'm fine. Losing sleep is second nature, part of our training."

"Liar."

"Okay, I give up. You want them to bring anything, honey?"

"I'm good. How about something for you for dinner. That might be nice."

"Nah, I can stop on the way home. But if you think of anything, you let me know, sweetheart."

While the hospital staff gathered all of the baby's things, Tucker called Steven Cook, who was delighted they were invited to the house.

With Brandy's bag, the huge bag of diapers and supplies given them by the hospital, and the bouquet of roses he'd sent, Tucker let the young assistant wheel Brandy to the Hummer. He called T.J. to let him know there was a chance he'd be a few minutes late.

Walking inside their home for the first time, Tucker was moved by how incomplete everything was. He vowed to wrap up everything he could, including the front yard project, even if he had to use credit cards to get it all done. She'd delivered two weeks early, so he felt a little like he'd been caught with his pants down.

"I'd really like a shower, Tucker. I didn't get one at the hospital this morning."

Tucker checked his watch and nodded, holding a fussing Kimberly while Brandy stepped into the shower. He could tell the baby was hungry, the way she twisted her nose and that cute little mouth of hers, punching herself in the face with her fist. He was still amazed at the miracle they'd created as he talked to her, walking her around the living room. Though she was large, as babies went, she still looked like a doll, so delicate and pink, and totally reliant on his love. Initially, he'd been nervous to hold her, even though he'd delivered babies during deployment and medic training at Ft. Bragg.

We got this, sweetheart. You go ahead and scream your little head off, 'cause Mama has the cure.

They heard Brandy's father pull up just as he handed Kimberly back to her.

"I think your dad's here, and I gotta go."

"Ah, that felt great. Thank you, Tucker."

"She's more than ready for you," he said.

"I can see," Brandy answered.

It was amazing how the baby seemed to know her mother's voice already. Depending on whether or not she was hungry, it either made her fussier, as her little face and mouth moved to the side looking for Brandy or calmed her down if she was satisfied. He'd been careful to speak to her in soft tones, not wanting to scare her, but the little one's ears were already attuned to the voice of her mother and paid no attention to him at all.

Like everything else Brandy did, she held a certain confidence, even though she was a new mom. Tucker didn't think he'd seen anything so beautiful in his life as the sight of Kimberly at Brandy's breast.

He gave a hug and kiss to Steven and Jillian and then dashed out the door.

CONGRATULATIONS WERE IN order when he got to the Team 3 building. Someone was passing out cigars, which Tucker had forgotten. In a matter of minutes, the air was blue with thick pungent smoke, like one of their poker nights. Tucker actually began to get a buzz on. It had been so long since he'd had a cigar.

He neglected to mention to anyone how hairy his daughter was, knowing how he'd get razed for raising a baby gorilla, like his mother had been when he was born. That was going to have to be on a need-to-know basis.

"Listen up!" boomed Lt. Commander Andrew Gibson. "Babies are a fact of life. You should know that better than anyone, Tucker, with your training."

"Yes, sir." The room around him sat to attention.

"Your kid is going to be teased about being raised by her grandpa," Gibson continued with a twinkle in his eye.

"Guilty as charged. I can see you've been there, sir," Tucker barked back.

The room instantly reacted as Gibson sported a cheerful grin. "You're damned lucky I like you, Hudson."

When Lt. Commander Gibson straightened up, he scanned his audience with deadly focus, causing everyone else seated before him to sit tall. All chatter immediately stopped. They waited.

"Okay, what we got here is sort of a mess. This op was planned before the huge wildfires that have destroyed so many acres on Gran Canaria, causing the evacuation of thousands of residents. There are fire-fighting units and extra Civil Guard from the other islands, Madrid, as well as some from Portugal—even a little equipment help from Uncle Sam. The place is crawling with police, fire, and rescue workers. It's like an anthill."

Gibson showed several videos of flames reaching into the night sky and flotillas of evacuees, as well as roving police units helping with the evacuation and the damage.

"We delayed a bit when the fires broke out. But this extra activity has stepped up the urgency. We fear some of those being evacuated are part of the smuggling operation. Or, they could be operating under the guise of a humanitarian aid vessel, trying to pick up new contraband. State thinks they could be attempting to unload some of their human cargo within the refugee population landing in Portugal, Spain, or other countries in the Mediterranean. Because of the emergency operations there, it's getting very dicey and, well, unmanageable. They're just not prepared for this type of widespread tragedy all at once."

Tucker could see a whole range of potential problems. The mood in the room had suddenly become quite glum.

"State has received intel there are even perhaps

American tourists caught up in the evacuation—either vacationers or long-term visitors to the island."

Lt. Commander Gibson turned off the video, and someone turned on the room lights.

"Gents, State is concerned about the possibility some U.S. citizens are caught up in all this and perhaps are being trafficked without their knowledge. That's why they've negotiated a short vacation to the Canaries, but only to retrieve our people. We can't touch or otherwise fuck with any islanders, anyone holding a Spanish passport, or a foreign aid worker who has diplomatic immunity."

Tucker knew before Gibson said anything further that they were on a tender leash.

"The problem for us is that while we're looking for our own, we'd like to rid the area of some of the bad guys with ties to Nigerian operators. We want to extract them quietly and hand them over to our Special Agent team for questioning and possible detention. We know some of them are there, because we've overheard conversations back and forth with one particular group we've been tracking in Nigeria."

He waited several seconds until the conversations before him stopped.

"We've got tourists, we got refugees from Africa who don't want to go back, we've got more arriving, and we've got people being evacuated. There's a list of names of certain individuals we are particularly interested in, and those are the only ones we want. Unless we walk into a hornet's nest. And with the history of this team, I'm not going to bullshit you to say it won't happen. We all know nothing happens like we planned, right?"

The general agreement on that point was loud and long.

"There's to be no fireworks. No blowing up buildings or causing any undue attention. And God forbid, no loss of life or even minor injury, especially to the Spanish or island population. If you don't know, you keep your hands off. Understood?"

Tucker nodded along with everyone else.

"There's a lot more coming, but I'm sure you have questions," Gibson barked.

"About how long will we be there, and when do we leave?" T.J. Talbot asked. He'd been mumbling, whispering things in Tucker's ear.

"Well," Gibson shrugged. "This is not a precise military operation, which sucks real bad. Never a good idea to not have a specific plan, but ours went up in smoke, so to speak, and now all hell's broken loose. We deploy in ten days."

Gibson was met with whistles as the group had been told it would be a month.

"Yeah, I know. Hurry up, then wait, then hurry up

again. It took longer to get our permissions because the Spanish and island governments were consumed with the logistics of this fire, and our mission wasn't really a priority for them like it is for us. So let me sum it up this way. Don't pay attention to the worker bees; find the queen. And we also know the longer we stay, the more attention we'll cause. So, we get in and out before we step in it—I'd say maybe be there three weeks. I hope less. Get who we can, send back information for something in the future, and get ready for next time. You all know this human trafficking thing is on the rise and is not going to go away."

Several men nodded. Gibson was dead serious, but his audience didn't reflect any of the tension they probably were feeling. Tucker knew this was how they'd been trained. He raised his hand and was called on.

"Sir, are we going to use the two assets we used before, Jean Douchet or Sven Tolar? Sven, in particular really helped us out."

"Yes, Sven will be on the team. He's meeting you guys over there. We're not sure about Jean. He's gotten a little entangled in Paris, from what we understand. We haven't approached him yet until we know for sure he's free."

"Is our platoon the only one going, sir?" asked someone from the back.

"Yes, at this point. I'll be going along with you. We have Lt. Jack Gridley, a Little Creek transfer, who's flying home from his honeymoon in Hawaii as we speak. So, without Kyle, we'll be fourteen enlisted men." He rocked in his shoes, eyes darting around the crowd, including making contact with Tucker. "We're expecting big things from some of you seniors."

The meeting was adjourned. T.J. snagged Tucker's arm.

"I guess we better get that fence built, don't you think?"

"Well, it will take a few months before she's walking or even crawling, but yes, I'd like to get that yard finished. What's your availability now?"

"I'm going to need to talk to Joe, and I'll see if we can get by there in the next day or two, if we won't be in the way."

"No problem. Thanks, T.J."

"How's everyone doing?"

"So far, so good. Kinda sucks I'll be gone so soon."

"I hear you, but at least you were around for her birth. With these short ones, you never know. Everybody healthy?"

"I got a sweet little pink daughter weighing over nine pounds, and her mother with enough milk to feed the whole hospital nursery."

T.J. squeezed Tucker's shoulder. "Good for you,

man. You deserve this. Then you can work on number two."

That left a smile on his face that lasted all the way until he got safely home.

CHAPTER 6

BRANDY GOT HERSELF up to make scones for T.J., Tucker, and Joe Benson, Shannon's father-in-law from her first marriage. Joe wore his carpenter's overalls and had brought two tool bags, with everything neatly organized, as if they were pieces of cherished antiques. So he holstered his hammer in the special loop created for it, took the pencil from behind his ear, and added it to the red and black crayon sticks lodged in his front pocket. His eyes were the size of basketballs as he lovingly accepted the hot scone Brandy presented to him on a paper towel.

"Why, thank you, dearie. You didn't have to go to all that trouble," he said and then took his first bite. "Oh man, this couldn't have come out of a box!"

She handed T.J. and Tucker each a scone. "It did. That's about all I can do when it comes to baking. Just my way of saying thanks."

Tucker gave her a kiss and a hug.

"She sleeping?"

"Of course, but probably not for long. With as much as she eats, she wakes up ravenous. But she goes right down when her belly gets full. She might be one of those who start sleeping through the night early," Brandy beamed.

"Larger babies are that way sometimes," added T.J. "Say, you don't happen to have any coffee in there, do you?"

"We have one of those one-shot machines. But I'm going to let everyone get their own. I gotta get back to check on Kimberly."

The men joined her and lined up behind Tucker, who prepared the coffee from freshly ground beans. He showed the coffee label to T.J.

"You get this stuff? These guys are former Team Guys. Their videos crack me up."

"I've seen them. Splitting beans with sniper fire. I've met them in Coronado too," said T.J. "Love the pirate on the front."

Brandy brought Kimberly into the kitchen, pulled up a chair, wrapped a small blanket over her shoulders, and showed Kimberly off to the men before she put the baby to her breast.

"Here she is!" gasped T.J.

"Now that's a pretty baby," said Joe Benson. "My wife, Gloria, would be right over if you ever need a sitter."

Brandy smiled and then focused on Kimberly's nursing, covering herself up discretely.

Tucker was telling Joe about his plans for the garden and what they wanted to do with the house, including their Brandy's thought to perhaps make a second unit upstairs.

The older man inspected the ceiling while sipping on his hot coffee and then studied the narrow stairway. He addressed Tucker.

"I think you should make that stairway into a closet or maybe a half bath, and add the stairs outside. You could protect it with an awning or overhang. Not like we have monsoons here."

"Joe is an expert carpenter, Tucker," added T.J. "He still does little repair jobs for several of our friends and his neighbors. But he used to build houses, right?"

"We'd build one, move into it, then sell it, and build another one. I think Frankie lived in about ten, maybe eleven houses growing up."

Brandy noticed a silence had fallen on the group and deduced it was due to the subject of Frankie's passing. Tucker had told her the story, but he delicately began to explain part of it again.

"Frankie is Joe's son, and T.J. and Frankie became best friends during BUD/S." Tucker's voice was soft and careful.

"I think I remember that, Tucker. Thanks."

T.J. added, "I was best man at his wedding when he married Shannon. She wasn't very happy with me for getting Frankie so drunk he passed out during the ceremony." The tall medic shook his head.

"That's my boy," sighed Joe. "He followed you around everywhere, T.J. You got him in a lot of trouble, but you were like brothers."

"That's a fact," mumbled T.J. "Frankie told me to watch over Shannon, who was over six months pregnant when he got taken out." T.J. was staring at his coffee like a psychic reading tea leaves. "I always had a secret crush on her, but I was a good boy. Being friends with Frankie was more important. At the beginning, Shannon didn't want to have anything to do with me."

"I heard all about that." Tucker grinned and toasted his coffee mug.

"Old Joe here kind of helped me break the ice a little. It was a very unselfish act I will never forget and could never repay," T.J. said, his words dropping off to a whisper. He wrapped his arm around Joe Benson's neck, making him blush.

The older man wiggled loose. "It just fit in place like a miter joint on a fine cabinet. I lost my son. You lost your dad. I think we were made for each other, T.J." Joe Benson blinked and rubbed something from his left eye.

Brandy couldn't remember seeing Tucker or any of his friends being so forthcoming with cherished emotional details. It touched her. After a short pause, Tucker cleared his throat.

"Think it's about time to get back out there, unless you two want to sit around and have a little cry." Tucker put his mug in the sink.

"Shut the fuck up," barked T.J. "Sorry, Kimberly."

Brandy put the baby over her shoulder and patted her back gently. Kimberly responded with a loud burp, which echoed throughout the kitchen.

"The princess has spoken!" Joe left his mug behind and followed Tucker and T.J. to the front door. He turned and waved at Brandy. "Thanks again. Those were tasty."

"I have more."

"Maybe later. Thanks."

He disappeared into the front yard filled with late morning sun. Brandy took the baby and sat, watching them from the living room couch.

Joe was the general.

THEY'D GOTTEN THE fencing up and decided to expand the project to cover the berm with redwood chips. They planted the two palms in the front corners of the property, to the left of the long driveway. The three men made furrows following the path of the sun but left a large square section untouched. She watched as Tucker noted things in a small spiral book. They shook hands, and before they parted, T.J. and Joe waved to her and gave a thumbs-up.

She hadn't moved from the large window in the living room. As Tucker entered, she said, "Looks beautiful out there. I like where you put the palms."

"Yeah. T.J. was right. It's the perfect spot. And don't know if you want to come out to see, but we left you a nice space up front for flowers or whatever you want."

"I saw that. And you've got the rows all lined up."

"Yup. Think I'll get the redwood bark and the veggie starts. You just tell me what you want to plant, and we'll get those puppies in."

Kimberly stirred, and Brandy adjusted her weight switching the baby to lie against her other side.

"Should I make you a sandwich?" she whispered.

"I'll do it. You're fine."

She followed him to the kitchen and sat at the table again. "You don't have to get those things today, do you?"

"No, but I'd like to finish." He stopped, his knife suspended in a jar of mayonnaise, his eyes dark and serious. "We don't have much time."

"I just want to spend as much time with you as possible before you go, Tucker."

"And I want to finish that garden, like I promised. You can look at it every day, water it, and think of me."

"How could I not think of you? I'd think of you if we lived in the desert in an old trailer. Everything makes me think of you."

Kimberly was getting fussy again.

"Think I'll go change her."

Tucker grabbed her arm before she could retreat to the back bedroom. "Hey, have I ever told you how much I love you?"

She kissed him. "Yes, all the time. But I'd love to hear more tonight after you've had a shower."

"Yes, ma'am." He picked up his keys, slipped his wallet into his back pocket, waved his goodbye with the hand not holding his sandwich, and was out the door.

She'd been waiting for their first sexual liaison to prepare a special meal, but tonight, she didn't want to wait anymore. This was the life she had, and it was special enough just being in his arms.

At first he wanted to be so careful with her, undulating inside, watching her face and asking over and over if it hurt. The third time he asked, she giggled, stopping him.

"I already told you, I'm fine. I don't want you to hold back. I want you to fuck me so hard I won't be able to think of anything else, understand?"

"You only have to tell me once, babe."

His enormous hands kneaded her flesh, his kisses turned her insides molten. He answered back her demand by changing positions frequently. His new question became, "You like that baby?" as he flipped her over and took her from behind. "What about this," he whispered into her ear.

She was left wet, gasping for air, wondering how in the world she'd ever be able to stand three weeks without him. Her last whisper to him was, "Mission accomplished."

HE LEFT ON a Tuesday, early in the morning. She noted he'd packed light this time, which she took as a good sign, meaning he wasn't taking any heavy firepower.

The sun was barely making it over the mountains to the east, and the area was bathed in a pink glow. The visions of their lovemaking last night was weakening her knees. They'd made love in the shadows, quietly whispering things she couldn't remember. It was more like an intense, goodbye kiss, a way to leave things on a positive note and wipe out the cobwebs of worry. It was something she'd learned how to do, to pretend that their life together would never end, while being realistic in the knowledge that he might not return.

She always expected a perfect outcome but prepared for the worst.

With Kimberly still fast asleep, she walked with him out to his Hummer in her nightgown, barefoot.

The early mornings were her favorite in the garden. The plants had started to expand, and some of the seeds she'd planted in the flower garden had begun to send up shoots.

He hugged her from behind while they both looked at the Tucker's handiwork.

"Enjoy your days out here, Brandy. I'm going to be thinking about you taking care of this little piece of heaven."

She turned in his arms and placed her palms up to his neck, stood on tiptoes, and kissed him while he gave her a firm squeeze. "You pay attention and come home to me, Tucker. I know you will, but I still want you to promise."

He held her hand at his heart. "I promise, sweetheart. Nothing will keep me from coming back to you both. Nothing."

He climbed up into the cab, started the engine, and backed out of the driveway, giving her a quick wave and a smile. She watched him, waving back until he disappeared behind the neighbor's hedge. And then she waited until she could no longer hear the motor.

If she had to choose, she'd rather have him home with her. She'd sacrifice anything except Kimberly to have him stay. But watering and tending Tucker's garden was going to help her get through it.

Until they could do it together again.

CHAPTER 7

TUCKER WAS GLAD to find Sven Tolar waiting for him at the Gando Airport on Gran Canaria. The former Norwegian special forces guy greeted the Team as they entered the hangar serving as their temporary Team building.

The metal building would be a good staging area for a quick exit, should that be needed. It also enabled them to receive supplies, including required firepower and devices, which could be subtly unloaded in small shipping containers and stored for later pickup.

A small tourist hotel that had been evacuated was to serve as their eventual living quarters once they left the safety of the airport region.

"My friend, how are you? I hear your little girl is beautiful!" Sven boomed as he gave Tucker a big hug.

"That's on a strictly need-to-know basis. You didn't get out there this summer. You owe me a visit."

Sven nodded and greeted the rest of the platoon as

they filed in.

"Lt. Commander Andrew Gibson. Nice to finally meet you, Sven," said Gibson as he extended his hand.

"Good to be here."

Tucker introduced him to Lieutenant Jack Gridley. "He's just joined us fresh off his honeymoon."

Sven shook the Lieutenant's hand vigorously and then commented, "Then you're a dangerous man, sir. You won't mind if I keep my distance?"

"Not at all," Gridley said with a wide smile.

Tucker liked their new officer and although it was his first deployment with their Team, thought he was a good decision-maker. He'd been a cop before he went to the Academy, and then became a SEAL, so he'd seen another form of combat that gave him some experience Tucker knew he could trust. They'd spent some time on the flight over getting acquainted. Normally, the two officers would be deferring to Chief Lansdowne, with his experience, though they outranked him. This time, part of that might fall to Tucker. Kyle was setting him up for a promotion and had told him so.

Light smoke still hung in the area, and the number of small-to-medium-sized planes had nearly quadrupled. Helicopters and light planes buzzed all around them. Sven noticed Tucker's focus.

"Way different than before, right?"

"I can see how easy it would be to have things slip

by." Tucker knew the appearance of order was an illusion.

"They brought in more than three hundred extra controllers and airport personnel from Madrid just to handle the extra load. They already have one disaster on their hands. No sense creating another one—something like a mid-air collision or worse."

Tucker helped stack boxes of equipment they'd brought. The men were all assigned to a corner of the building where two dozen cots were set up, along with a makeshift mess and two bathrooms. A small trailer Tucker recognized as portable shower rooms had been brought in. Sven selected a cot next to Tucker's. T.J. was on the other side of him.

He stashed his duty bag under the cot, sat, and accepted the bottled water and sandwiches being passed out to all the men. His first bite signaled that he was long past due for a meal, and his stomach churned. But the hard roll containing a meat and cheese mixture was still delicious, and he'd devoured it in four bites.

"You stay in touch with Kelly?" Tucker asked Sven, cleaning his palate with water. Kelly Fielding was their State Department Special Agent liaison, as well as being the sister-in-law of the American nurse they'd rescued.

"She never returned any of my calls or emails. I'm giving her some time. You guys get together with Riley at all?"

Tucker imagined the two palm trees planted in his front yard. "At the hospital up in Redding, and then he sent us a housewarming gift. But no, we've not been in touch."

He decided not to say anything about Riley's offer to work with him again. He suspected perhaps the old man had made a similar offer to Sven. That left him with a question he was dying to ask.

"Is he a part of this one?"

Sven shook his head. "No, I don't think so. I mean, did you take a look at that bucket of bolts you flew in on? Even your naval transport planes are better than that thing. He'd have never sent you on a Spanish charter."

That confirmed what Tucker had been told by the two officers.

"Well, perhaps after this caper, you'd be due for a visit in Portland. I imagine Kelly'd like to see you."

Sven shrugged. "She'll reach out if and when she's ready. I don't chase women anymore."

Lt. Commander Gibson called a meeting, instructing them to stay comfortable. Most everyone stayed seated on their cots, readying themselves for an early turn in.

Gibson held a pile of papers in his left hand and started to pass them out.

"I need you to memorize all the faces and names on this sheet and take a picture of them on your cell phones, because we can't take these out of the building. I've got six targets identified who, as of two days ago, were still on the island. A number of them work at the Capri night club in Las Palmas. It's nothing special, a dance club and bar. It caters to foreign tourists. The rest of them are listed by last known address, or work affiliation, or neighborhood."

"Holy shit, we got a *General Two Fingers* here!" said Fredo.

Everyone looked down at the smooth-shaven black man with dreads, bearing a medal of some kind over his left breast pocket. All the other pictures except one looked like a rogue's gallery from some casting call in Nigeria, of mixed races and varying degrees of tooth possession.

One guy was crisply dressed in a white linen suit and had red hair and horn-rimmed glasses. Tucker read his name, Jens Vandershoot. His last known whereabouts was the Tradewinds Hotel in downtown Las Palmas.

Tucker and T.J. shared a look. T.J. rolled his eyes and mumbled *great.*

"There's also Red Arrow Employment, which they've been watching closely now for nearly a year. It's a domestic help employment service, specializing in placing nannies and domestic temporary workers with wealthy, mostly European families vacationing or with temporary residency here."

Calvin Cooper raised his hand. "Sir, operationally, how do you want us to do this?"

Gibson looked at Tucker. "I think you can split up into teams, just coordinate and share. No, we absolutely don't want the whole Team to descend on the dance bar or one location, if that's what you're thinking."

Everyone laughed.

"Are we allowed to dance?" asked Lucas.

"You can't dance, so the answer is no. And I sure as hell don't want to listen to you Karaoke, either," shouted Alex.

The Team erupted in laughter again.

Sven stood up. "Coop, most of you were here before. With everything going on, I don't think we'd attract too much attention if we stayed in groups of two or three. Is that what you mean, Commander?"

"More than likely, we'll find other areas to look for these guys once we start the visual," added Gibson.

Someone asked, "So are we limited to just these on the list? What if we find someone else we know's involved in the human trafficking?"

"That's a good point," answered Gibson. "For now, these are the only ones we're cleared to mess with, per our instructions from State. But you know what can happen. So let me be clear. You don't fuck with anyone else and then find out we've made a mistake, okay? We're on borrowed and very limited time. If everything blows up, we'll have completely destroyed our mission and the valuable intel assets State has in place. We play nice. Tough but nice."

Gibson went over other logistical items, and then the meeting was adjourned. As the group broke up, T.J. turned to Tucker.

"I've always been told I play nice, right, Tucker?" He followed it up with a smirk.

"My favorite way to be," he answered.

Fredo and Coop had joined their circle.

"Is it my imagination, or is every mission now more complicated than the last one? More rules, with just as much danger, but so many ways things could go all wrong," said T.J.

"The nature of the evil we fight is adapting and changing," added Coop.

Everyone nodded full agreement.

"When I was active, we always said we were working with the other units, but unless we were working with you Americans, we pretty much ran the show," said Sven.

Tucker didn't like the level of negativity being expressed. "Well, it's what we're trained for—to do the impossible so no one even knows we were there. War is changing, gents. The enemy is mobile and doesn't look like a soldier anymore. He could be a businessman, a truck driver, a clerk, or storekeeper. He speaks more languages than we'll ever know, and he moves in and out of multiple countries. He doesn't play by the rules, but we have to."

"Well said, Tucker," Coop whispered. "We use our experience and instincts, and we keep the information close."

"Roger that," several others responded.

TUCKER APPROACHED LT. Commander Gibson. "I forgot to ask in the group if we could call home. I'm assuming there's enough static out there that it would be okay. But can we get through?"

"You'd be right. Not sure about the connection, but I do have a sat phone, if you need it. But not outside this building, and I'm not sure if the metal will interfere, but go ahead and try and then let me know. I'll announce it."

"Thanks."

Tucker dialed Brandy and did get her voicemail so left a brief message that they'd arrived and he was headed for bed. He warned her about what she already knew—that his calls would be infrequent and not to worry. And of course, he told her he missed her and the baby more than he wanted to think about.

He waited for a shower, got all the traveling sweat off his body so he could concentrate on some restorative sleep, turned on his small book light, and added to his journal.

Wondering what the hell I'm doing here with a beautiful wife and baby at home who need me. Not complaining, but boy is it different now coming here as a father. One saving grace is that I know somebody's kids are being trafficked, and if I can do anything to help stop it, I'm going to. We have a tight window and parameters, but the mission is clear, and we're not here to fight or blow shit up. Not saying it couldn't happen.

The island is crawling with ants from every country. At least from the air, that's the way it looks. I'll know more tomorrow.

Like any long travel, I'm anxious to get out and move my body around. I can't run or swim in the ocean to get rid of the jitters, so I'm hoping we get to do a lot of walking, trying to be invisible.

Glad I brought my good sunglasses.

I'm kissing you right now, honey. It's kinda tight, but you're gonna share my cot tonight and help remind me of my real purpose in life until we can do the real thing.

You never answered my question about how

many. Was it two, three, or four? From where I sit, any one of those answers would be good. Hell, even ten would be fine. As long as some day they help me in and out of my wheelchair!

Tucker thought of Mr. Riley in his squeaky machine. He was rich, and he was disabled. And probably cut off from most of the world except for people or experiences he could buy. But he still lost his son and nearly lost his daughter.

That wasn't going to happen to the Hudson family. It had nothing to do with money, either. He wondered if Riley felt he controlled his empire or if it was the other way around.

A part of him felt sorry for the man.

CHAPTER 8

B RANDY GOT TUCKER'S message when she came
home from her first outing with Kimberly. It had
been a simple store run, but she brought way too many
things for the baby. In the end, she realized she'd get
much better streamlining and preparing in advance for
these trips.

It warmed her heart to know he'd gotten to the Canary Island destination.

Christy Lansdowne, Kyle's wife, called to tell her
the ladies on the Team had arranged to bring her hot
dishes, or salads. Someone would be stopping by each
day until she called a halt to it.

"The way I hear it goes, people get their refrigera-
tors so full a lot of it goes out in the trash, but at least
you don't have to do anything."

"Thanks, Christy. I ventured out myself this morning. I have to get much better at this before I'll do it
again."

"Wise decision. Let us take care of you a little."

Brandy was grateful for the help.

She'd gotten into the routine of watering the garden with Kimberly strapped to her tummy, if she was awake. The two of them had meaningful one-way conversations. She explained what they'd planted and what she was doing, every single step.

Tucker had left the name and phone number of his former Teammate who had the teenage daughters. Although they'd failed to get together with the family before he left, she decided she'd initiate a meeting. At her last checkup, her pediatrician told both of them it would be safe to bring Kimberly out in public.

She set up a visit, stressing it would be a very short visit and not a dinner, the next day, in the afternoon, when the girls would be home from school.

THE TANNER'S HOME was in a newer area but farther from the beach and downtown traffic. Geri was at the front door before she could ring the bell.

"Oh, look at her! She's such a beautiful baby, Brandy. And she's huge."

Brandy wondered how she managed to keep her trim figure after having four kids, but Geri was nearly model skinny. Inside, the girls were seated on the living room couch, all in a row. She nodded to each of them.

"Bryce isn't home—got something he had to do at

the base, so I'm not sure he'll make it, unless I can convince you to stay for dinner."

"I better not, Geri. Thanks, though."

Brandy nestled down on the couch between the four girls. The youngest one moved in front and kept to her knees, peeling back the blanket to inspect Kimberly' fingers and toes.

"You want to hold her?"

"Yes."

"Keira, go wash your hands first," commanded her mother.

The six-year-old ran to the kitchen and scrubbed her hands and arms to her elbow. That prompted one of her sisters to do the same. The two oldest girls snickered.

"Make room for your sister," Brandy softly requested. The girls parted and the little one sat beside her, while Brandy handed Kimberly over. "There you go."

The youngster's eyes became wide as she looked at her mother. "This is so cool," she whispered.

Geri laughed, clasping her hands together. "I've got to take a picture of this!" She ran out of the room in search of her cell.

The oldest girl produced a phone she'd been sitting on and snapped a picture. Geri returned and took pictures of the whole group of them together.

71

Brandy fielded questions for several minutes, but when the baby began to wiggle and then cry, little Keira immediately passed her off.

"She's just hungry, that's all," Brandy explained.

Geri added, "And she probably knows the difference between someone else and her mother. Babies are very smart."

"I want to hold her," said Shelby.

Brandy bounced Kimberly gingerly, hoping she'd calm down, but lay her in Shelby's arms anyway. "She's not going to last long, so don't feel bad. She's really waking up now."

And that's exactly what happened. Brandy took her back and placed her on her breast to feed.

A gasp emanated from the two youngest girls. Brandy smiled at their mother. "They're adorable, Geri. What a nice family you have."

Mrs. Tanner was near tears, her face beaming. "Tori, Lynne, you remember when we brought Keira home from the hospital? You remember all this?"

Keira was checking her phone again. Geri tried to grab it from her hands, but her daughter sat on it.

"I've turned it off," Lynn said defensively.

"Honestly, your dad is going to be more than displeased when I tell him. I don't understand all this texting."

"Just kids from school, Mom. No biggie."

"But this isn't what we do when we have company. Your friends can wait." Geri's agitation was escalating.

"Tori, go take Shelby and let's serve Brandy with some ice water, okay? And bring some for me and everyone else."

"Roger that," Tori said as she extricated herself from the couch, pulled Shelby up, and left the room.

Geri gave Brandy a puzzled look. "I'm just glad they don't pick up on any of his other lingo. And he has some choice ones."

"I'll bet. So does Tucker." Brandy turned to Lynn. "Do you babysit?"

"Sometimes." She shrugged and stared down at Kimberly with her chin balanced on her open palm. "Does she use a bottle?"

"Not yet. I'm pretty much it for now."

"You have a pump?" Geri added.

Brandy didn't quite know how to respond. "Not ready yet. I'll wait until Tucker gets back. Just one of those things I didn't think about."

"Well, that's good you haven't needed it. I did with my first one."

"I'm right here, Mom. Lynn, remember?"

Brandy was shocked at the attitude of the teen and started to cross her off the babysitter list, when Lynn added, "Just kidding. I have to give you a hard time, you know that. It's what you do to me all the time."

Geri and Brandy exchanged a look. Brandy didn't say a word.

Later, the girls watched her change Kimberly's very messy diaper, examining the yellow-green contents and scrunching up their noses.

"She's got hair like boys," remarked Keira.

Brandy chuckled as she put the sleeper back on, wrapped the baby loosely and placed her over her shoulder for another burp.

"You should see her daddy. She takes after him."

The girls laughed while their mother delightedly looked on.

Brandy decided to bring up the subject of babysitting, explaining it would be some months, but asked Lynn if she and Tori would like to watch Kimberly together some time. They were both enthusiastic about the possibility.

Brandy didn't want to stay too long so began to gather her things to leave.

"Can I bring anything for you? How are you doing with cooking?"

"The ladies on Team 3 have been overdoing it."

"Yup, that's what we do all right. You let me know, though."

"Will do." The two hugged again.

"Here, Keira, take this for Brandy," Geri said as she handed the diaper bag to her daughter.

They said their final goodbyes, the girls waving to Kimberly's unfocused face over the top of her shoulder, all the way to the doorway. Keira walked with her down the steps and back to the car, watching Brandy strap the baby safely inside.

She handed back the diaper bag.

"Thanks, sweetie. That was fun. Do you like babies?" Brandy asked.

"Yes, but my dolls are teen dolls now. No babies." Keira was shy and so blurted out, "She smells nice."

"Yes, she does, doesn't she?"

A cloud came over her face as she spoke, "Lynn has a boyfriend. She doesn't want Mom and Dad to know. She texts him all the time. They would be super pissed if they found out."

Brandy was surprised with the reveal. "Really? Maybe you should tell them. What do you think?"

"Oh no. My sister would kill me. I can't do that."

"Well, think about it. If you think it's wrong, you should—"

"I don't like the picture he sent," she interrupted.

"What picture?"

Keira looked at the front door and saw the coast was clear. "He sent her a picture of his pee pee!"

Brandy arched up and made a mental note that somehow she was going to have to meddle, and she didn't like being in that situation. She didn't want to do this without talking to Tucker first, since it was a relationship he valued. This was going way beyond her babysitting needs. And that already short list had just gotten much smaller.

She leaned over and spoke softly close to Keira's cherubic face. "Keira, you know that's wrong. It's always wrong. You should tell her so the next time you see or hear about it. And you really should tell your Mom or Dad."

Keira's eyes grew wide and filled with tears. "I shouldn't have told you. Now you'll tell my parents. I'm going to get in a lot of trouble."

She turned and quickly ran back into the house, slamming the front door behind her.

Brandy's heart ached as she watched Keira disappear. She wanted to go back inside and let Geri know about the conversation, but the anger and concern had clouded her judgment, and she needed Tucker's opinion before she opened up that box of horrors. There would be no good way this could work. Geri and Bryce needed to know. Keeping everyone "happy" was the least of her concerns.

If the situation were reversed, she'd hope that someone would tell her the truth about what her kids were doing on their cell phone. She knew it was not only the right thing to do, but it might keep Lynn out of harm's way.

She drove home, pondering her decision, hoping that Tucker would agree with her. She missed him more than she ever had.

CHAPTER 9

TWO DELIVERY VANS showed up at dawn to pick up the team. They were to be transported to their new lodging, now set up and ready to go, where they could unpack. Then they'd divide up into smaller groups for their forays into town. State had hired a small team to help with their meals and logistics. A portable surveillance tower was installed, and they'd have direct communication with Washington for updates.

Gibson had received word that several cell phones were being tracked with the CIA "hairnet" device, giving them the opportunity to identify and monitor phone traffic, as well as pinpoint specific locations. Three additional hand carry devices were given to the team; one went to Tucker, Gibson kept one, and the last was given to Fredo.

Even at daybreak, the road into Las Palmas, located north of the island, was jammed with other delivery trucks, lorries, and buses. They passed emergency trailers, and staging areas loaded with pallets of supplies, and tents of varying sizes, including temporary hospitals and housing for displaced citizens, tourists, and workers. Tucker doubted their vans would wind up on anyone's radar.

They also passed several international relief organization mobile units, fire and rescue vehicles, and a fair number of media trailers. Seaside resorts were overrun with troops, transport trucks, and relief workers. It appeared even tourist buses were pressed into service. In the distance were spires from a dozen or more cathedrals.

Several large ships, including a cruise ship, were docked in the main shipping and industrial zone. In addition, hundreds of smaller vessels moved in and around some of the littler ports. The scale of the operation was massive, and with the proximity to the other seven islands making up the Canaries, as well as the eastern coast of Africa, the whole place resembled a large space station. It was the hub of a wheel involving dozens of countries and cultural differences, many of whom were closer in distance than Spain, the country they were part of.

The two vans snaked their way through the back streets of the city just as shopkeepers were readying for the day. Several school buses and black SUVs also fought for space. Once they cleared the capital, they turned sharply and began to climb into the hills, closer to the remnants of the fire, which had consumed thousands of acres and a huge national wildlife preserve. As the smoke got thicker, the buildings became less frequent and the temperature cooled. Several villages along the road appeared abandoned but were blocked by barriers, guarded by the local Civil Guardia in blue uniforms armed with semi-automatic weapons. Gibson had told them looting had been a problem in certain evacuated areas, and the Guard took their jobs seriously, being tasked with keeping order.

The view east, down toward the Atlantic Ocean, was spectacular as bright blue glimpses of it popped up through the dark smoky clouds. Rain was threatening, which actually would improve conditions on an archipelago known for a lack of annual rainfall. But with forty thousand acres smoldering from the raging wildfire, even mudslides would be welcomed.

When the smoke cleared, they were protected by winds coming off the bright blue ocean. At a distance, it looked like a colorful free-form patchwork quilt. Colorfully painted houses with flat roofs dotted the coastline and crept into the hills, shoved up against large boulders and outcroppings of jungle foliage.

At last, they came to a set of massive gates and stone columns protecting the approach to their lodging. A crudely made wooden sign attached to the façade indicated the property was closed. The first driver exited the car and entered a code into the communication box at the left of the gate, and several seconds later, the lumbering structure swung to the side, allowing them entry. The grounds beyond were lush, landscaped with flowering trees and tall grasses, bordering both sides of the crushed stone driveway leading downhill. In various locations along the way, tips of tall trees appeared to have been damaged by fire, green leaves turned into curled pieces of brown scrolls. Most of the landscaping and roadway was covered in light grey ash, as flakes swirled all around them, reminding Tucker of the first snow in the Sierras.

The stone and plaster hotel was tucked into the hillside with a spectacular view of the ocean and nearly all the coastline down to the airport. Tucker wondered if it had been a grand home at one time because it looked several hundred years old. The tall, ornate façade extending up three stories in the middle, like a crown. From here, they could see just about every ship or airplane coming on or off the island.

This area, thankfully, was completely free from smoke.

Sven paused on the patio outside the lobby, taking a quiet moment, his pack slung over his right shoulder. "I stayed here a long time ago."

"Oh yeah? When?"

"Gosh, nineties—late nineties. Overstayed my visa and nearly got married, too." He scratched the back of his head and re-hitched up his pack.

"She was a Spanish lass, then?"

"Oh yes, very Spanish." Sven sighed. "Knocked me right off my feet. Her parents were very wealthy, lived in Madrid. She was going to school here, studying art."

Tucker didn't want to pry, so he walked slowly beside his Norwegian friend as they climbed the painted tile grand stairway and kept his mouth shut. His background hadn't been anything as dramatic, or as romantic, until he met Brandy. He wanted to know more but knew Sven might enlighten him on his own.

"I'm never going to tell my new bride about this," started Lieutenant Gridley. "She'll think I did it on purpose."

"Yeah, but you were in Paradise, man," said Trace. "No fires, no bad guys, and it was your honeymoon."

"I think Trace is right," said his brother-in-law, Tyler. "This is nice, but I'd still choose Hawaii any day."

"You know they got a volcano on the other island?" added T.J.

"And snow," said Fredo.

"How the Hell did State find such a place, Gibson?" asked Cooper. "You must've pulled some mighty big strings."

Lt. Commander Gibson disagreed and barked back, "Not on your life. Just the luck of the draw. That's all it is." He stood his ground on the lobby floor as he studied the men climbing the stairs, examining the old wooden beams and unique carvings. Then he added, "Figure out your roommates. When you're done, come on down here for a chat in about an hour. That's when the food arrives."

"You taking one of the rooms up here, Commander?" Tucker asked.

"Already picked out. It's the one with all the crates in it."

Tucker knew Sven wanted to bunk with him, and he didn't mind. He'd picked out one at the end of the hall, next to the fire escape.

The rooms were huge, covered in crude paver tiles bordered with colorful hand-painted tiles used as baseboard and door trim. He didn't like the fact that he and Sven had to share a bed, albeit a king bed.

"Shit," he whispered.

"I was thinking the same thing," mumbled Sven. "I was so anxious to get the best view I didn't check out the sleeping arrangements."

"Let's see if there isn't a spare after everyone's situated."

Sven disappeared and returned with his report. "All taken. We got by far the biggest room, and even better, we got a desk and a bigger bathroom with a tub."

"Damn, and here I didn't bring my back scrubber and the salts." Tucker punched him in the arm. "You really think we'll have time for a bath, man?"

"Soaking in steaming water is a national pastime where I come from."

"Yeah and rolling around in the snow afterwards."

"Do you see any snow?"

"Good point. So if you're taking too long in the tub and I gotta use the john, I'm not waiting, but I won't look," said Tucker.

"Fair enough," answered Sven. "And I won't tell anyone we spent our days here in the honeymoon suite."

Tucker stiffened. "Say what?"

Sven pointed to the heart-shaped pillow on the bed Tucker had failed to see. Sven was starting to unpack. Tucker just threw his bag in the corner, his irritation burning a hole in his stomach.

"You tell anyone about this, you're dead."

"Got no one to tell." Sven's smile was evil, and when he wiggled his eyebrows up and down, he looked like an old Viking bastard straight out of the movies.

Tucker normally would have moved his journal under his pillow but now didn't want to risk its discovery, so he left it in his bag. He considered calling Brandy.

"Did the Commander say anything about using our cells?" he asked.

"I think he said we could, just not in town, unless it's work."

"I'm going to try to contact Brandy, if you don't mind. She should be getting up about now."

"Tell her I said hi." Sven pointed to the bathroom. "Taking a shower."

Brandy picked up before the third ring. He could hear Kimberly fussing in her arms. "Hello, sweetheart. How're my girls?"

"Oh Tucker, I was hoping you'd call. We're good. Staying busy. Let me get her situated, and then I can talk." She lowered her voice as he heard fabric and movement. "I'll have to whisper. She's already starting to figure out there's a whole world out there."

He waited until she came back on the line.

"There, all better. How is it over there?"

"Can't say much. I'm going to write it all down, like I did before. But I have to say the accommodations we've been scoring are first class. Am I making you jealous?"

"A little. So you're in another villa or something?"

"Sort of like that. Anyway, long trip. Same old, same old. I'm rooming with Sven, and he says to tell you hi."

"Give him my best. Does he know about the baby?"

"Yup, knew before I could tell him."

"You guys. Nothing gets by any of you. He going to go back to Africa?"

"I don't know. We didn't get that far. So what have you been doing? Can't stay long, but just a quick update, okay?"

"Actually, I have to talk to you about something. I was over at your former Team Guy's house. You know, the Tanners?"

"Oh, good. Sleuthing for sitters?"

"Started out that way. But I need your advice. I think I know what you're going to say, but I need to hear it from you."

"Is there a problem?"

"How well do you know them, Tucker?"

"They only had two when I served with him. I didn't see the family at all. Is she okay? Something going on?"

"Not Geri. It's her oldest daughter, Tucker. She's fourteen. And she's texting guys on her cell phone."

"Hardly a national tragedy. Happens all the time, Brandy."

"No, I get that. But her little sister said the boy was sending her pictures of his junk."

Tucker wasn't sure he'd heard Brandy correctly.

"Did you see it?"

"Oh Hell no. What do you think I am?"

"Well, you going to take the word of a little girl of, what, five?"

"She's six."

"Well then—that makes all the difference."

"Stop it, Tucker. I believe her. I feel like I should tell Bryce and Geri about it. Now, this could be like you implied, just a sister fight, or maybe she likes to tell stories. But think about it. What if Kimberly came home and told you this story? Would you believe her? Would you want to tell the parents of that child?"

Brandy was right, but it was damned hard to relinquish control over the situation. If he were home, he'd just jump in his truck and drive over there and get to the bottom of it. He thought Bryce would probably want to know, just like he would.

He remembered seeing the older girl transfixed with all the messages she was getting, and Bryce's reaction to it. He was going to have to trust Brandy to make that call to his friends. And if need be, he'd clean it up afterwards. It saddened him that they hadn't exercised more control over their daughter.

But Brandy was right. It was not okay to let it slide until he got home.

"Wow, you've got a tough one there. I think your instincts are correct. You need to tell Bryce and Geri. If he's got a problem with any of that, have him call me, okay?"

"I'm going to tell him we talked about it first. Can I say it was your idea, to protect their daughter?"

"Yes. Do that." He didn't hear a response and wondered if the phone call had been cut off. "Brandy? You there?"

"I'm here. I'm going to call them this morning."

"Please don't mention it to anybody else. That's their family thing, and he's not even on my Team anymore. They'll want to keep it quiet."

"Oh, absolutely. I wouldn't dream of it."

"So you let me know." He tried to think of something light-hearted to say to her, but his insides hurt. It underscored how vulnerable children and women were all over the world. And here he was all the way over across the Atlantic. Too far away to protect his own little family.

He thought about Colin Riley. He thought about how that man had suffered when his daughter had been trafficked. How he missed all the signs by his own admission. He saw himself reading that damned card and dreading to find a spot for those trees to root and become a permanent part of his little kingdom.

It would be impossible to ever really get away from all that. Everything was connected in a strange thread of human existence. He could tell himself differently, but it would be a lie. Then he thought of something.

"How are those palm trees, Brandy? You keeping them happy?"

"They're loving it here. You were right. They do feel like guardians. They keep watch over my garden. My sunflowers are already six inches tall. The cabbage and the broccoli are doing great. Not so much the lettuce. Too late for tomatoes, I think. But we'll have flowers all through the holidays. I love it so much, Tucker. Thank you."

"I'm glad. That makes me happy."

Sven exited the bathroom followed by a cloud of steam.

"I gotta go get cleaned up for dinner. Leave me a message on that other thing, and I'll try to call back tomorrow. No promises, though."

"I understand. Good night, Tucker."

"Night, Brandy. Kiss my angel for me."

"She kisses your back."

Tucker shut off his phone and placed it in his bag.

"Everything okay?" Sven asked.

"Nothing big. Just a tough call she's got to make this morning. I wish I was there to do it for her."

Sven left him alone, turning his back and getting dressed. Tucker dashed to the bathroom, tore off his clothes, and stood under the lukewarm shower, letting it wash off his worry.

Trying to make himself feel better, he mused that he was only about fourteen hours away. A couple of plane rides.

But he felt like he was on the dark side of the moon.

CHAPTER 10

BRANDY LAID KIMBERLY down while she showered. She made coffee and a little oatmeal, staring down at the slip of paper Tucker had written Bryce Tanner's cell phone number on. She knew she had to do it first thing, or she'd get caught up in the day. She wanted to make that call while Kimberly was asleep, and she'd not have any interruptions.

It was going to be one of the most difficult things she'd ever done. Could she trust herself with the truth? Did she hear it wrong from little Keira? Was there just a sisterly spat going on she was about to step right into? Would they say it was none of her business?

But the risk on the other side just wasn't worth it. What the younger sister had told her was wrong. It wasn't the sort of thing a six-year-old would just say out of the blue, which is why she believed her. And what was her reward for being honest? She'd feel like everyone was out to get her, that there wasn't anyone there to protect her.

She'd studied sexual assault in college. What she could remember from her studies was that it always started out innocently. And the unlucky ones lived in families where things either went unnoticed or unsaid. The lucky ones were when someone spoke up, questioned something that didn't sound appropriate.

And this was one of those.

She rinsed her dishes and placed them in the new dishwasher. She poured herself another cup of coffee, checked on the baby, and found her still sleeping soundly. She closed the bedroom door, sat down in the living room with her coffee mug, and dialed Bryce's number.

It went directly to voicemail.

She disconnected. For a second, she felt relieved, until she realized she'd have to keep trying, because that was just the right thing to do.

So she dialed again. This time, she left a message.

"Hey there, Bryce. This is Brandy Hudson. Say, I have something I need to talk to you about and I'd really like to talk to you sooner rather than later." She left her cell number and hung up.

Her hands were shaking, so she took an apple to help satisfy the churning in her stomach. She vowed not to have another coffee this morning, picked up a magazine, and waited.

She'd dozed off on the couch when her phone rang.

"Hey, Brandy. This is Bryce. How are you?"

"I'm good."

"You talk to Tucker yet?"

She panicked, thinking perhaps Tucker had called him instead of waiting for her to do it.

"Yes, they got over there. All fun and games, and you know I can't say more than that."

Bryce chuckled. "I deserved that. So what's up?"

"Well, this is a very difficult call for me to make. If it wasn't for the fact that I have Kimberly here, I really should talk to you in person, but I didn't want to wait."

"This sounds serious. Is there some problem with Tucker?"

"Oh God, no." Her nervous laughter sounded ridiculous. She was rethinking all her motives, her perceptions, and trying to blank out that she promised Tucker she'd make the call.

He had paused and was waiting, and she knew she'd feel horrible about sticking the knife into his gut.

"I'm afraid I have something I need to talk to you about that disturbs me. I—I wasn't sure, so I want you to know I talked to Tucker first. It was his suggestion I call you," she lied.

"You're scaring me, Brandy."

"Okay, here goes." She took a deep breath and began. "The other day when I was over at your house,

Keira helped me put my things in the car. Geri had scolded your oldest about using the cell phone, er— getting text messages she was answering while I was there."

"God dammit all to Hell. I'm going to take that damned phone away."

"Well, I agree with you, Bryce. And here's why. Keira told me that Lynn was getting messages and pictures from a boy. Her boyfriend, she said."

"Boyfriend? She doesn't have a boyfriend."

"I think she does—or, at least, Keira thinks she does. And maybe Lynn doesn't. Maybe Keira made it all up. But here's the thing. Keira said she somehow saw pictures of the boy's *thing* that he'd sent to Lynn."

Bryce was breathing hard into the phone. Brandy knew how hard her words must be to hear. "Go on. What else?" His words were terse, and she could feel rage beginning to boil underneath.

"Keira's very worried you and Geri will find out about it. And she's worried her sister will hate her for telling me. Heck, I think they'll all hate me now. I can't say why, but I believe her, Bryce. I don't know her or your family, but I just get the impression she's not lying. She didn't say it like a joke. She trusted me with that reveal and then quickly tried to backpedal it. I guess that's what makes me believe her. Do you understand?"

"I don't want to. I wish you'd said anything else but that. I wish you'd told me my kids did something to you or the baby or said something mean. Any of those things I could take. But this—" His voice trailed off, and Brandy's heart plummeted to the floor.

"Like I said in the beginning, I didn't want to make this call, but I thought I had to. Both Tucker and I thought you should know so you could check it out on your own. I pray it's all wrong, and it's just been a horrible misunderstanding."

"Keira never lies," Bryce whispered.

"Oh Bryce. I'm so sorry."

"No, you did the right thing. As much as a part of me hates you for this, it was the right thing. I don't think I'll ever be able to look you or Tucker in the eyes again."

"But maybe it's not—"

"I had a funny feeling when all these text messages kept coming in, but I thought it was girls at school. Some of those girls can be a little wild. She wants to fit in. God, I hope she didn't feel pressured or—"

"Is there anything I can do? Please tell Geri she can call me. I'll see her anytime she wants."

"No, I've got to get hold of Geri, and then we'll get that damned phone and see for ourselves."

"If you feel it's appropriate, if you discover it's the truth, please tell Keira, if you want to—from me—that she's very brave. If you think it's appropriate."

"Thanks, Brandy. This is the last thing I wanted to do today, but Geri and I will talk, and I'll let you know, if you want."

"Oh, please. I hope I'm just having a good old-fashioned postpartum emotional meltdown. Honest."

"I'll bet. But you did the right thing. Tell Tucker you did the right thing. We'll investigate and probably get the police involved."

Brandy felt drained after the phone call. She sat in stunned silence, not even wanting to go outside to water the garden. Her heart ached. Her arms and legs felt heavy. She hated to trouble Tucker while on his mission and wished she'd been strong enough to make the call without his advice. But they always shared everything with each other. That was just the way they did things. She hoped that Geri and Bryce discovered it was some prank played by one of Lynn's girlfriends at school, but even that wasn't right.

She took several deep breaths and closed her eyes. She tried to feel Tucker's arms around her.

And then the baby cried and washed away all the pain.

CHAPTER 11

THE TEAM HAD been issued used packs so they wouldn't draw attention. Just about every one of them was different, and some even looked like used children's school bookbags. Fredo's was more like a full tool bag, since he was tasked with bringing some small flash bombs, which he had strict instructions *not* to use, Invisios so each group could communicate with one another, and some tiny tracking devices with super glue sticky backs. These would be issued as needed. He also had wire cutters, both copper and aluminum wire and a tiny chain link bolt cutter Fredo and Coop were enamored with.

"Where the hell did you get these?"

Stuart Bonilla, one of the team who met them first at the house, answered, "I bought that in the Ukraine last summer. Very handy. Even works in freezing temperatures."

"I've seen those. Very useful," Sven Tolar offered.

State had hired twenty-five-year-old Bonilla, a crack radio guy, from smack dab in the middle of Ohio, borrowing him from one of their intelligence contractors. Stuart had spent quite a bit of time in eastern Africa growing up doing mission projects sponsored by his church. He had relatives who ran a mission school for girls in Benin, so he was familiar with many of the eastern dialects from Benin and Nigeria, and he spoke fluent Spanish and Portuguese.

Stuart showed them how to work the hairnet device, to track and capture cell phone signals so he and some of their brothers in Virginia could trace not only where the cell phone was traveling but what numbers it called. It was no bigger than a pack of cigarettes or a cell phone battery. He demonstrated how it worked with his own cleared cell, showing how it tracked a call he made in front of them to Gibson's cell.

"Now it will tell us who Gibson calls and so forth."

"Is there a way of masking this so the cell can't be picked up?" Tucker asked, examining the little black box.

"Not unless it uses something other than WiFi or Satellite. If it sends or receives a signal, it will pick it up."

"Short wave?"

Stuart wiggled his outstretched fingers to show that it was wonky. "Problem with that is that we know the signal is sent, but the bandwidth of anyone who receives it is too broad. Kind of useless. We want portal-to-portal signals. That's what we track."

"You must get a lot of data to cull through," remarked Gibson.

"We have computers upstairs that filter what we want. Yes, at the end of an hour or two, the screen looks like a spider's web. We look for patterns and movement, not actual conversations. That's not to say Fredo here won't be helping us out with some listening devices. Most of the smaller ones I've given him won't detect all the way up here, but we couldn't chance all this clunky equipment getting discovered. Plus, it's not very portable, so you'll only listen in when we have to. Great for hostage negotiations."

Tucker didn't like the sounds of that.

"You have to be worried about accidentally detonating a bomb?" asked Cooper.

"Yes, we do. Therefore, we don't *send out* a signal unless the bad guy is carrying something we want to detonate before he gets it placed. In that event, it can be kind of a weapon too. You want to make sure you don't do that, okay? It also makes you visible if other guys have some form of cell tracking."

"And what are the odds of that?" asked Tucker.

"In the states, with high-level drug dealers, they're very wise. They use burners and switch out SIM cards all the time, so you lose the trail. Mob crews in Europe and Asia do too. We're thinking we have a leg up here. They might know about them, but they haven't grown in their business acumen, so to speak. We got a tech advantage, gents."

It was obvious to Tucker that Stuart was rather proud of his equipment.

"You three carry these very close to your body, and only take them out when you use them. And you better bring them back."

Gibson asked that each man put a shirt and water into their pack, *not* their wallet. "Take something to jot down notes and a pen. Some sunscreen and whatever personal items you need. Make it look legit. No firepower. Sorry. Your weapons stay here."

Several of the Team grumbled, mouthing words like feeling naked without their favorite sidearm. Gibson wasn't making any exceptions.

"We're going in a little cold. You get caught and have a piece, you're probably going to be out for the rest of the mission, maybe longer. Just not worth it."

"I'm taking my slingshot."

Gibson didn't know Danny's story and gave a whimsical look. "Whatever."

Tucker was going to bring his NV binoculars.

After lunch, everyone readied themselves for the daytrip.

"Keys are in the vehicles, boys," one of Stuart's men blurted out. "Have fun and be careful out there."

TUCKER RAN FOR the Jeep before anyone else could claim it. The house had come with five other older-model cars and two pickups, all designed to help the men blend into the local population. The cover they'd designed is that they were firefighters from different jurisdictions in California, all friends, who decided to take vacation days to assist the island's population in the cleanup and recovery efforts. They were helping a friend tear down an apartment building. It was meant to look like an impulsive, self-funded operation to steer away from the concern they were connected to any government entity or had military background.

That would also leave things open for a little bar-hopping and making inquiries. And as firefighters, they wouldn't be expected to get too heavily involved in drinking and doing drugs but might get introduced to some things on a limited scale, recreationally.

In other words, they were going to pose as heroes with somewhat tarnished halos, who didn't want to cause trouble and lose their livelihoods back home. And they wouldn't be expected to know everything about the island like a frequent tourist or local would.

Calvin Cooper eyed the Jeep longingly. "Only for today, Tucker. Then you can have this old thing tomorrow."

Coop's mode of transportation was going to be a wine-colored 4-door pickup import that was missing the front bumper and had one tire that had been spray-painted green, for some reason. The front bench seat was ripped and could give anyone in shorts a nasty cut.

Tucker gave him the finger. "I rather think that suits you."

Two squads were to stay back at the motel, which included Lt. Commander Gibson, so he handed Coop another portable "hairnet" with the admonition, "Don't you lose it, Coop or you'll be walking."

"And that would be worse. Come on, Coop, let's beat them down the hill," said Armando as he jumped in the front passenger's side.

DeWayne Huggles did an adequate job of nearly filling the entire second seat. Through the open window, he banged on the roof with the palm of his hand. "We go!"

Off they went, in a cloud of smoke.

Tucker swore that he'd let them get ahead of him and, with Sven and T.J., sped out the driveway, spewing flakes of ash in their wake.

Fredo and Danny took another older dark blue semi-compact with a large rubbed-out circle on the hood where someone had unsuccessfully tried to wax the vehicle with the wrong product. As they turned around, Jameson jumped in behind them, along with Jack Gridley.

Tucker was working like Hell to catch up to Coop's truck, but when he spun out on one of the gradual turns with a downward slope, he lost traction, which caused him to fan the brakes carefully until he slowed. He squeezed and let go his grip on the steering wheel until he felt more comfortable with the vehicle. He could feel T.J.'s eyes on him, but no one said a word.

"You see who got the sat phone?" T.J. asked him.

"That would be Jack," answered Sven.

The others stayed behind.

Coop got out first to punch in the code, and as the gate opened, Tucker's Jeep was able to slip by him and take over the lead.

Sven put his hand on Tucker's shoulder. "They have horses here, sometimes in the brush. Be careful, my friend."

"Good to know," Tucker said, as he slipped his sunglasses down from his scalp. "T.J., see if you can find some country music, will ya?"

Sven fell back into the seat, laughing.

NEARLY TWENTY MINUTES later, at the bottom of the hill switchbacks, they ran into the edge of the capital proper. He pulled over, parking behind a hardware and auto parts store.

"I'm noticing something different right away," whispered T.J. as he watched the other two vehicles join them.

"Different? Different than what?" asked Tucker.

"I'm not seeing as many dogs and chickens as on the mainland. But man, there are tons of cathedrals here."

"Big Spanish influence," said Sven. "You should see the ones closer to the city center. Really does remind me of Madrid. Wide streets, lots of churches. Bells ringing all the time."

"Not as many children here, either," T.J. added.

Tucker had noticed the same thing. A few children dressed in their school uniforms moved in and around the long lines of traffic, sometimes holding hands in a line. But not nearly the ones they'd seen in Benin and Nigeria. "Maybe because of all the rescue operations."

"Maybe they've already been sent elsewhere," said Sven.

Tucker knelt in the shade. It was hot already, and although he had a sleeveless shirt under his short-sleeved wrinkle-free golf shirt, it was one layer too many.

He turned on his cell phone and scrolled over the pictures of the six men they were to find.

"Anybody got a preference what position to take? We got the Red Arrow, the Tradewinds, and the

Capri."

"I think I could use a little umbrella drink, so I vote we go to the Capri, Tuck."

"That sit well with you guys? Who wants to take the employment agency or the Tradewinds?"

"We'll take the Tradewinds," requested Danny. "We got four, so it would be easier to hang out in the lobby or whatever they have.

"Okay, that leaves the Red Arrow for you guys," he said to Coop.

DeWayne Huggles had a question. "Tucker, how the hell is this black man gonna go into the Red Arrow employment agency and go looking for a maid? Did anyone think about that?"

"Maybe you're looking for a temporary job, Huggins," said Cooper.

"Oh, you mean, like being a chauffeur. You see any big black limos hanging around taking rich folk out to dinner? You mean that kind of employment? No, sir. I don't think so. That's a bad idea."

Tucker needed to calm Huggles down. "Maybe today you just watch, record who comes and goes. Look for something you think should be investigated. Look for bad guys or guys who look like they don't belong."

"That's the problem, Tucker. *We* don't belong. How the hell am I going to figure out who else doesn't?"

"Did you take your meds, Huggles?" Coop interrupted.

Tucker was going to laugh until he saw Coop being entirely serious.

Their sharpshooter from Mississippi closed his eyes, "Dammit." A few seconds later, he whispered, "Forgot."

Tucker looked at Lt. Gridley. "Your call, sir. This is a call you get to make."

Gridley stared down at his sandals. Anyone with any kind of military background would spot him for an officer. Even while dressed down and casual, he still was the best-pressed and cleanest of the bunch.

Time to show what you got, Gridley. You've got to earn their trust.

"He goes back and gets his meds. We don't put the rest of the team in jeopardy because you forgot your meds."

"Good call, L-T." Tucker saw Gridley stand up straight and throw his chest out.

"Coop, you'll take them back. And I'll tell you what...you get to have the Jeep on the way home tonight, fair?" said Tucker.

"That's a good trade."

Tucker watched the three of them blend in with the slow-moving traffic north. He approached his Jeep as T.J. and Sven hopped in. He gave Jack a thumbs-up, and the foursome broke off, heading into downtown in the little blue import.

"What are the odds they got some George Strait at the Capri?" he asked T.J.

"Who's George Strait?" asked Sven.

T.J. spoke to the side of Tucker's face. "I'm not even going to dignify that question."

CHAPTER 12

JUST AFTER LUNCHTIME, Geri Tanner called Brandy and asked for a call back. Brandy was outside walking the garden when the call came in. Luckily, the phone didn't wake the baby.

"Hey, Geri, what's up?"

Geri's voice was scratchy over the phone. It sounded like she'd been crying.

"This has been a heck of a day. The kids were all in school when you talked to Bryce—and—"

Brandy interrupted. "I'm so sorry, Geri, about all this. I hope you don't think—"

"No, I understand. That was a tough call to make. I wouldn't have wanted to do it. But I have to thank you. We went through Lynn's things in her room, and she's got some pretty disgusting pictures."

"Pictures? Keira didn't say anything about that."

"I'll bet not. Keira would have told us immediately. I have no doubt about that."

"What kind of pictures, Geri?"

"It didn't look like some of her friends, but I don't know. Some were tied up; some in their underwear. It was hard to recognize anybody. One girl had a gag around her mouth. Stuff like that."

"Oh my God." Brandy didn't know what to say.

"Bryce has a friend on the San Diego police force, and he says we definitely have to make a report and get that cell phone to find out who did this. They don't want to spook whoever it is there at the school, so we can't just show up and make her tell us and get some kid arrested, but we're definitely going to bring in the police. I just don't want to cause a big scene for her. It will hurt all the girls. But this boy is a real creep with some serious problems, and we've got to get her away from him."

"I agree. But I'm relieved to hear that you're getting the police involved. That's what should be done. You have any idea who this kid is?"

"Nope. Not one picture of his face. Just pictures of girls. And they're young, too."

"Younger than Lynn?"

"I think so. One of them didn't have a shirt on, and she was prepubescent. I'm guessing about twelve. Bryce's friend was disturbed with all of it."

"I can imagine. So what's the next step?"

"Well, I wanted to ask you for a favor. I pick up

Keira in a little bit. Shelby and Tori have a full day, like Lynn. But I was wondering if Keira could come over and stay with you for a little bit, maybe a couple of hours, until we get Lynn interviewed. I'm having my two other girls go home with one of their friends' mother. They have no idea what's going on. We're not going to interview Keira just yet. Hoping we can get information and cooperation from Lynn, first."

"You know, Libby Brownlee is a part-time marriage and family counselor. She's Coop's wife?"

"I don't know her."

"She'd be someone really good to be with Lynn when she's interviewed."

"They use a special social worker, child's advocate here. But maybe for something in the future. Right now, I feel like I need some counseling. I just never—"

Geri broke off, crying.

"No problem, Geri. Oh, I'll do anything to help out. Can you drop her by? Only wrinkle is I know she's going to be mad."

"She doesn't know we know yet. I'd just play it like that. Say Bryce and I had an appointment and we had to rush her over to your house. We thought she'd like to play with the baby. That sound okay?"

"Anything you want, Geri. Oh, I'm so sorry about all of this."

"Me too. Just what we get to do. On top of all this,

Bryce is supposed to do a temporary deployment in about two weeks. Timing sucks."

Brandy was heartbroken Geri would be alone with the four girls, having to deal with possible police action and interviews.

"You know, you can have any or all of them come stay with me any time. Or maybe you want to take some time together, just the three of you, before he goes. I'll happily take the three girls for a few days. It will give me something to do, and I think they'd be a big help."

"Really? Well, I'll talk to Bryce. I couldn't ask you to do all that, Brandy."

"Think about it."

"I will. So I'll be over in about a half hour. Remember, you don't know anything."

"I got it, but do you think Keira has told her about the conversation I had with her in your driveway?"

"I don't think so, but I'm not sure. Keira's been very quiet. Lynn took her cell phone with her to school, which she wasn't supposed to do. We looked for it in her room and couldn't find it."

Brandy knew that little Keira, once she found out that her mother knew about her secret, would have one more reason not to trust her.

Right after she hung up, Joe Benson called to say that he had two retired friends he wanted to bring over, and if she was okay with it, there were a couple of things he wanted to work on in her yard. He also wanted one of his friends to look at the roof and the stairwell and help figure out if putting stairs on the outside would be feasible. His friend was a retired engineer.

"Well, Joe, I'm babysitting a six-year-old this afternoon. Her dad served with Tucker, so I'm doing them a favor. But I think it would be okay. I've got tons of food here."

"I'll have my wife get some sandwiches, and she can drop them by later on, so you don't have to cook. Anything else you need?"

"Oh, gosh no. You'd be doing me a favor helping me to get rid of some of these casseroles."

"Do you want her to bring Shannon over and perhaps Courtney? She's five, you know. The two girls are about the same age."

"That's a terrific idea, Joe! Go ahead and ask her."

"Okay, well, I'll see you within the hour."

It was going to be a full afternoon. But it would help keep her mind off how much she missed Tucker.

GERI WALKED DOWN the driveway, holding Keira's hand. She'd brought a small suitcase with a change of clothes and nightgown, in case they were late getting back.

Brandy knelt down to greet the child.

"I've been looking forward to seeing you again, Keira. Kimberly is about to wake up. You want to help me change her or maybe give her a bath?"

Keira wouldn't make eye contact. She buried her head in her mother's skirt. Geri's eyes were puffy and red, and she hadn't put on any makeup.

"Come on, sweetie. Mommy and daddy will be back before you know it. Come be a big help with Kimberly," Brandy tried again.

"I don't want to go," Keira said meekly.

Brandy stood, gently brushing hair from her face, and then tapped the top of Keira's head. "We'll have fun, you'll see. Do you have any favorite movies I can put on the TV?"

Keira turned around, still leaning against Geri's legs, but delivering her answer like it was an order.

"Frozen."

WHEN JOE AND his buddies arrived, they carried a large crated box that appeared heavy enough to need a 4th man. Struggling down the driveway, Joe asked for directions to the back of the house.

"What do you have there?" Brandy asked.

"You'll see. Now, can I get to the back through a side gate, or do I have to come through the house?" he asked again, out of breath.

"You have to come through the house. The side yard doesn't have a gate."

"Well then, that's another thing we'll have to fix. You have to have a gate there," he said, shaking his head. She cleared a path at the front door and allowed them to walk in front of Keira, through the living room, and then through the kitchen and out the back-sliding glass door to the overgrown yard there. Keira didn't take her eyes off the movie or even seem to notice the men and their cargo.

Joe and his buddies set the large box against the backside of the house. With his hands on his hips, Joe surveyed the space.

"Honey, you don't have a rear-fenced yard."

"I know."

"Why the devil did they build a fence with no gate but not have a fence to protect the backyard?"

"The neighbor told us that someone behind us used to use this property as a cut-off and used to drive through."

"What? That's completely ridiculous."

"Apparently, he'd done it for many years. The owners had the fence built to stop him."

"That's not very neighborly," said one of Joe's friends.

"Oh, Brandy, this is Sy Woods. And Tom Nettles."

As she was greeting them, she heard the baby crying. "Duty calls."

Kimberly had hiked her shirt up over her shoulder and was waving her free arm back and forth, unhappy being uncovered. She was probably hungry too.

Brandy decided against interrupting Keira, so changed the baby and then brought her into the living room, taking up a seat next to her temporary charge.

Keira moved to the side, giving her more room on the couch, without removing her eyes from the big screen. The baby began to feed as Brandy watched the movie.

She knew it was going to be a long day.

She was only halfway there.

CHAPTER 13

T HE CAPRI WAS the type of bar that could have existed in nearly any country in the world. The first thing that hit Tucker when he walked through the beaded entrance was the smell of alcohol, which meant they didn't wash the floors very often.

Coming from the bright mid-afternoon light into the dark and dank hole that was the bar hurt his eyes. The name, painted on corrugated metal, with a pink flamingo wearing a necktie, was a total misnomer. There wasn't much that reminded Tucker of Capri, of the Caribbean, or Florida, where flamingos lived in the wild and weren't tended in multi-million-dollar landscaped gardens.

It was just a bar, and a dirty one at that.

The floor was sticky as he made his way to a table in the corner covered with dirty glasses. Sven and T.J. pulled up two chairs around the table and stared back at him.

Tucker grinned. "I'm thinking no country music."

"You'd be one hundred percent correct," T.J. agreed.

"Doesn't look much like the Capri I remember," mumbled Sven, looking over his shoulder at the multicultural array of bodies hugging up to the bar like baby piglets getting suckled.

A tiny dance floor with blinking colored lights was empty, but Tucker spotted several scantily clad ladies hanging on customers in the periphery and figured they were probably the only ones who danced.

A woman washing down the next table asked, "You want some-ting?" in a heavily accented African dialect Tucker didn't recognize.

"You have beer?" asked T.J.

"Yes. Bottles."

Before they could ask what their choices were, she left, returned a few seconds later, and placed three unlabeled brown bottles on the table, opening them one at a time. They were not chilled.

T.J. examined it before he placed it to his mouth. "Beer?"

"Yes. Boss beer. Only kind." Her dark coffee-colored skin was covered in a fine sweaty mist. She had red nail polish, chipped, and deep purple lipstick on her full lips. "That's nine Euros."

Tucker gave her a ten-dollar U.S. bill and another

five on top of it. Her eyes flickered slightly as she grabbed it off the table.

"Tanks."

They watched her head for the bar and whisper something to a rather rotund man with a thin moustache and an earring in his left ear. He wore several ornate rings and gold chains. His light-colored silk or rayon shirt stuck to his sweaty body. The waitress disappeared behind a doorway.

Sven examined his bottle like it contained ant poison. He looked to T.J. to get some encouragement. "How bad is it?"

T.J. had drained half of the bottle and set it before them. "I'm trying to figure out what they fermented here. It definitely wasn't hops or barley."

Tucker didn't want to taste his now.

"Oh, I think there's enough alcohol to kill whatever it has, but it's got a taste that's hard to place. Go ahead, Tuck. I think it's harmless, but probably very high in alcohol."

Tucker timidly sipped the bottle, after wiping the top off with his shirt. It wasn't sweet but had a honey-like aftertaste. He could feel the first few swallows travel down his parched insides, and it reminded him he'd better get something in his belly.

As his eyes became more accustomed to the darkness, he noticed a dusty collection of what looked like

Voodoo dolls displayed above the lighted mirror behind the bartender. He counted over thirty, and there were no two alike. Some were made from straw, some from rags and yarn. Some had painted faces, and nearly all of them had hair. Upon closer inspection, the hair didn't look like yarn, but human or animal hair.

A chill slipped down his spine.

"Sven, you know anything about Voodoo?"

"Only what you told me when we were on the mainland." He turned to face the bar, following Tucker's gaze.

"Well, that's kind of creepy," whispered T.J. "Looks like some kind of admonition or something. Not very welcoming."

"Did you see the hair?" Tucker asked.

T.J. took a second look. "Like I said, creepy. I really didn't need to see that."

Tucker was aware they had attracted the attention of the bartender, who now waddled over to their table.

"Ah, the Americans have landed. We are all now saved! Praise be to God!" His English was good, and he appeared comfortable speaking it. "You wish that I bring you another beer?"

"Boss beer?" Tucker asked.

"Yes. Yes. Boss beer. Very, very good beer." He placed his palm to the middle of his chest. "I am Diego, the boss, and I make it. All natural. No preservatives."

Tucker didn't think there would be any. But he foraged his question. "What's it made from?"

"Maize, corn, you know, corn on the cob?"

"You make beer from corn. I didn't know that could be done," said T.J.

"You like it?" the bartender asked. "Corn is very, very good for you. It has a sweet taste, no?" When no one answered him, he shrugged. He looked behind him, scanning the room quickly. "You are here for work? Vacation?"

"We're here to help out a buddy. We're firefighters. He's had some damage we're helping him with. Clean up," answered Tucker.

"Ah, I see. Very good. Well, if it is your first visit to our little island, let me introduce myself and make some suggestions, okay?"

Tucker decided to play along.

"First, may I suggest you be careful about the food? And watch for bandits. Your wallet, understand?"

They nodded.

"Only eat food in reputable establishments. No carts on the street, understand? It will make you sick. Watch out for the little children who pickpocket. And the gypsies. And also stay away from the police, you know, the Civil Guard. No not get into a traffic accident, at all costs."

T.J. interrupted him. "Is there anything here we *can*

do for fun?"

Diego's face widened, his smile showing off several gold-rimmed teeth. "We are known for many things, but at the top of our list is our lovely ladies. I can arrange some introductions, if you like."

Again, Tucker agreed to go along with Diego's line of thinking.

"We might be interested. But we're both, except Sven here, we're married men."

"The girls are very discrete. Very, very nice. We are a melting pot of Spain, Portugal, and Africa. Ladies from every country with very different tastes and talents." His eyes were glowing, his fingers itching with anticipation for the money he was thinking he would make.

"Well, we probably need to finish our work for today. When should we check back with you?" Tucker asked.

"Tonight would be good. The ladies come later in the evening, when we have more customer, you understand?"

They nodded.

"And you are single, yes?" Diego asked Sven.

"I am."

"So you can really play the field. You like experienced ladies?"

Sven, in spite of all his worldliness, was seriously

embarrassed. He stumbled with his answer. "I like them pretty. But not too old." He took a quick glance at Tucker, and it registered what Sven was doing.

"Oh, yes. Young. Perhaps you like them young, then?"

Tucker's stomach lurched. Noticing the cell phone hitched to Diego's belt, he reached into his inside shirt pocket and slid the hairnet switch to on. Diego was intent on listening to Sven's answer and didn't notice.

Sven acted like this was news to Tucker and T.J. "Sorry, fellas. But, yes, I like them on the young side. Not children, of course." He scowled.

"No, no, never. But I understand completely. You like them fresh and untouched," he enunciated like he was reading off a delicacy from a menu. "This is always more expensive, but not impossible. I can also arrange that she come cook for you, keep house? She can be your wife while you are here—working."

Tucker could feel T.J.'s tension explode, noticing the veins in his neck protrude. He was also grinding his teeth.

Sven answered, "No. I don't need a wife. I just want to have fun."

Diego laughed, causing a couple of the bar patrons to turn around.

"Then fun you shall have, my friend. Your new friend, Diego, will see to it personally."

Two men darkened the doorway, and Diego immediately disconnected to give the newcomers his complete attention. Both were dressed in slacks and long-sleeved shirts rolled up to their forearms due to the heat. One wore a loosened tie, as if he worked in a bank or was in business locally. They were lighter in skin tone than Diego, with a mixture of Creole and Indian features. Neither took their shades off as Diego brought them to the opposite side of the room where no one was sitting. While the three discussed something private, T.J. retrieved his cell and snapped photos of the group.

"You still on?" he asked of Tucker.

"I hope so."

"I recognize one of those men from the photos," said T.J. "I think we just widened the net."

CHAPTER 14

T HE MOVIE ENDED, and Keira wanted to go outside to watch the workmen, who were causing noise with their drilling and sawing. Brandy wrapped the baby tight and escorted the six-year-old out the sliding glass door and onto the patio. All of a sudden, she discovered what they were doing.

Bits of packing material and remnants of the original box lay on the ground off to the side. In the middle were several large pieces of painted plywood, bracing and a scattering of Joe's tools, including a skill saw. Joe was studying a sheet of directions he'd laid out at his feet just beyond where Brandy and Keira stood.

He looked up. "Surprise. Bet you never would have guessed."

To Brandy's amazement, Joe and his friends were assembling a playhouse kit. As the walls were raised onto the flooring material, Keira turned to her, suddenly more excited than she'd been all afternoon.

"It's a playhouse for Kimberly. Oh, you're such a lucky!" she said, bouncing up and down to look at the sleeping baby.

Brandy sat on one of the patio chairs so Keira could watch the baby sleep.

"Joe, I can't believe it. Where did you get all this?" she asked.

"Bought it from a friend I know who sold his toy store. I used to put them together for him, and he said he had a couple left over still in the box."

"It's pink," shouted Keira.

"It sure is, little lady," answered Joe. "We're going to have it up here in about a half hour. You want to be the first one to play in it?"

Keira was bouncing, cheering, running back and forth on the patio. Brandy asked her to stay away from the tools and equipment.

The doorbell rang, so Brandy walked back to answer it.

"Oh hi, Brandy. I'm Gloria Benson. I don't think you remember me, but I'm Joe's wife. Charlotte's grandmother." The attractive woman held a shopping bag.

"Nice to see you again. Come on in."

"I brought some sandwiches and iced tea for the boys. Joe was so excited to come over today, Brandy." She wrinkled her nose and whispered, "It gives him something to do."

Brandy took the bag offered, placing it on the kitchen counter. Mrs. Benson followed right behind her, focused on the baby.

"Well, hello there," she greeted Kimberly, who had just opened her eyes. "She's a perfectly beautiful baby."

"Here," Brandy said as she allowed Mrs. Benson to hold her.

"Oh, it was such a short time ago Charlotte was this small. I miss those days," she said as she made faces with the stoic Kimberly.

"Did you bring her over? I'm watching Bryce and Geri Tanner's youngest, Keira."

"I'm afraid not today. My husband thinks he can arrange the world in a matter of seconds. They already had plans." She looked back down at Kimberly. "Tucker must be over the moon with delight."

"I don't think he ever thought he'd have a child."

"Oh, nonsense, men can have children at any age. We're the ones with the expiration date."

Brandy saw that Gloria Benson was someone she could trust and was easy to befriend.

"You have to go for more," Gloria added.

"This is about all I can handle at the moment." A shadow passed over her as she thought about Geri and her four daughters. Mrs. Benson returned the baby.

Keira opened the slider and announced, "Look,

Kimberly, your house is almost finished!"

The men finished putting on the window shutters and the front door. They tightened the screws with Joe's screw gun, while they cut extra trim pieces for the door frame and outside windows. They also created a ledge so that the kitchen window had a pass-through on either side. Joe held the door open, and Keira ran inside without fear, screaming in delight.

The work crew sat as Mrs. Benson brought them their iced tea and sandwiches. She knew them and their dietary likes and dislikes well, flirting slightly with each one. She also brought out a peanut butter and jelly sandwich, but hesitated.

"Can she have this?" Gloria asked.

"I think so." Brandy asked Keira, "Honey, can you have peanut butter and jelly? Does your mommy let you eat those?"

"Only strawberry. I only like it with strawberry jam."

"Well, what do you know. I got it right!" Gloria chuckled and handed it over. "Can I get you something, Brandy?"

"Water. I'd like a glass of water. The glasses are in the cabinet over the dishwasher."

Kimberly was wiggling, so she propped her up to sitting position on her knee and burped her. Keira was fascinated with trying to catch the baby's attention.

Minutes later, the men gathered up their tools and Joe took the leftover box remnants to his truck. Gloria said her good-byes, while Joe and his friends began discussing what should be done with the stairs to the upper great room. They measured, drew small sketches in a notebook, and looked for locations of studs in the walls bordering the stairwell. They went outside and measured the side of the house, called numbers to each other on sizes of windows both downstairs and up-stairs, and measured the length of the side fence.

Keira was beginning to get in the way, running up and down the steps and weaving around the men. Brandy managed to get her attention, reading some of the books her mother had packed in the suitcase. She fell asleep on the couch.

Brandy put the baby down and then checked her phone for messages but found none. It had been nearly three hours, and she was hoping for an update. Then the phone rang.

"Geri, is that you?"

"Yes. Listen, it's not going well here."

"What's happened?" Brandy whispered, moving into the kitchen.

"They took her phone away at school. She was caught texting."

"Oh, dear."

"She got it back when school was over, but then she

dumped the phone in the drain, Brandy, before we could reach her."

"Oh no. So now what?"

"Bryce's friend says they want to interview Keira. Lynn argued that this boy is in love with her and wanted to meet her. That's what she told us. She told us she didn't want him to get in trouble, so she threw the phone away."

"Wait a minute. You said he was one of her friends from school." Brandy's heart was racing.

"That's the thing. Now she says she's never met him. She says she found the pictures at her school and denies he ever sent them to her. Begged us to just throw them out. I know she's lying, Brandy."

"Of course she is. She's protecting him. Boy, this guy must be good."

"Well, Bryce's friend says we don't even know if it's a guy or who he is. But she's convinced he loves her."

"I can't imagine how you feel."

"Have you ever heard anything so insane? My daughter—" Geri's tears took hold.

Brandy let her cry. When Geri blew her nose and seemed ready to listen, she asked, "So what can I do?"

"They want to bring someone over to your house to question Keira, since she's the only one who saw the cell phone pictures. They think it would be better to do it at your place, rather than our home. Keira might feel less self-conscious."

"Whatever you want, Geri. I'm here for you guys."

Okay, let me get back, and I'll give you a call if we're coming over. In the meantime, can you give her some dinner? Maybe get her ready for bed in case we're late?"

"No problem. She had a sandwich late this afternoon, so I don't think she'll be hungry. I have chicken noodle soup. I have mac and cheese, tons of other things in the refrigerator."

"Perfect. Thank you so much."

"What about Lynn?" Brandy asked.

"I'm dropping her off at my mom's. They've asked that I keep the girls separated for now until we can get them interviewed."

Brandy dialed Tucker and got his message line. Her heart was banging so loud in her chest that she thought she might get sick.

"Tucker, I'm having one of those good and bad days all rolled up into one. Kimberly and I are fine. We have a new pink playhouse in the backyard, but the whole world around us is going crazy. God, I need to hear your voice, Tucker. I'm trying my best, but my world just isn't the same without you. I realize that more and more every day. You should be here with me and the baby. Forgive me, because I know how selfish that sounds. I shouldn't be telling you this, but I just have to get it off my chest. And I'm scared. I don't feel safe."

She watched the sleeping form of little Keira and realized how vulnerable they all were.

What would Tucker do?

"He'd stick it out, make it work," she whispered to herself.

Of course. It was the obvious solution to a problem that couldn't be solved, except with the passage of time, because it was impossible to control. He'd watch and look and wait for the opportunity to be a hero. He'd stay focused and alert to all the forces. He'd never give up.

He'd protect them all.

She decided to just focus on that.

CHAPTER 15

TUCKER WISHED HE'D asked more questions of Stuart Bonilla when he was getting the hairnet demonstration. He didn't want to pick up meaningless information. There was no telling how many cell phones were located in the bar. He counted thirteen sitting on stools and bet every one of them had a device of some kind.

So he reached back inside his shirt and turned the switch off. If he caught either of the two newcomers answering their phone or making a call, well, he could reverse that.

"I think you need to get closer to them," Sven whispered.

Tucker looked at the back part of the dance floor and located a men's restroom. He again activated the device and announced, "Gotta take a leak."

He grabbed his unfinished beer bottle by the neck and sauntered past the three gentlemen. Just before he reached their table, he stumbled, dropping the bottle and following its roll until it hit Diego's shoe.

He didn't have to work hard to feign being tipsy. He'd shared most of Sven's beer with T.J.

"Gawd, I'm so sorry." He pressed too familiarly into Diego's side and didn't make eye contact with the newcomers, who both stood up and backed away, moving like powerful cats. Tucker immediately assessed they'd had some serious martial arts training. Their stares were hostile.

"Hey, don't touch me, friend," Diego said, pushing Tucker hard. "You can't just walk up to me in a meeting."

"I'm sorry, man. I thought you could get us more beers, that's all. I'm on my way to the head."

"Sonja!" Diego barked, while his two other associates quietly slipped their hands into their pockets where Tucker was sure they carried some sort of weapon.

The waitress appeared from around the curtain and scurried over to take Sven and T.J.'s order. Tucker raised his hands with a wavering "don't shoot" stance and sidestepped his way to the restroom.

The cracked mirror revealed what a hot mess he was. His nerves were on edge, and he had two days of stubble, which itched like crazy.

What the fuck am I doing here?

In case he was being watched, he used the John, leaning his elbows on his thighs and trying to calm himself. He rubbed his scalp vigorously, sighed, stood, and washed his hands. He swung the door open and nearly collided with one of the Creole gentlemen, who again backed up two steps to avoid having any contact with Tucker.

The man's smooth skin was nearly feminine, and Tucker noticed he wore just a touch of eyeliner and blush, which was something he never expected to see here. His dark hair was plastered down flat on his head, every hair in place. His cold black eyes emanated pure evil.

He was grateful for the gap between them so there would be no chance the device would be detected, yet he moved slowly so there would be a better chance for a signal to be captured at such a close proximity. Tucker eyed the ground, mumbled a, "Pardon," and then returned to the bar.

Sven and T.J. were ready to leave. T.J. suggested they head over to the Tradewinds and try to rendez-vous with Lt. Gridley and the other three men. Tucker was going to jump behind the steering wheel when Sven slapped him on the upper arm and pointed across the alley.

The Tradewinds was less than two blocks away. It had been a nice hotel at one time with ornate balconies in wrought iron like Tucker had seen in the French Quarter in NOLA. It looked to have been built in the late eighteen hundreds and was plaster over wood construction with stone retaining walls and fireplaces. It didn't take much to envision Europeans from all over sitting on their balconies, sipping cool drinks and looking out at the blue Atlantic while the rest of the world went by. He felt the ghosts of escaped pirates and fugitives from government—perhaps several governments, as well as the dangerous liaisons and secret political meetings. This place was made for clandestine operations.

It always would be.

There was a quiet order to this place, he thought. Control was an illusion. He knew if he had to spend any time here, he'd wind up going native, which would mean one thing—he was back to a solitary life again where he didn't have to worry about anyone but himself. And his Team buddies.

"Tucker, want me to call Fredo?" asked T.J.

"Sure, go ahead. Tell them where we are."

A pile of crates was stacked just across the entrance to the hotel, nearly obstructing a narrow alley with clotheslines hanging from windows on the second and third floors facing the other stone and brick buildings across the small space. He imagined this was a natural form of air conditioning because very little light managed to carve out a spot.

He sat, swearing because he'd forgotten to turn off his device, and did so. T.J. had just hung up.

"They're still in the lobby. Not much happening. Most the rooms are being used by rescue workers and some foreign press," he said.

Sven checked his watch. "Should we gather up everyone and go back?"

"Let me find out if Coop's men are on their way."

His call was answered on the first ring. "Thought you'd be shooting me a message, Tuck," said Stuart. "Good job. We've got a ton of stringers out already and logged in nearly a dozen connections to phones on our target list."

"Good. I was wondering if I was too far away."

"You were just right. I've got some solid tracks going on now. We'll be busy tonight."

"Are Coop and the guys on their way down?"

"Gibson nixed that. You seven are on your own."

"Okay, we'll text when we leave. Just wanted to check."

"You did good."

Tucker was going to suggest they head into the lobby and pick up the other squad when, all of a sudden, their two visitors from the Capri walked past, forcing them to duck into the shadows of the alleyway. The men stopped at a sedan parked on the opposite side of the street, opened up the trunk and took out a large suitcase. After searching both ways on the street, they entered the hotel, wheeling the suitcase behind them.

"Call him back and tell him to get the net on," he said to T.J.

He didn't want to risk being detected so waited against the cool bricks. The noise from the edge of the busy city echoed off the walls, exaggerating the sounds of trucks, bulldozers, heavy equipment, scooters, and the sounds of horns blasting at the harbor. There was nothing familiar to him. He breathed in and out slowly and waited for his body to calm down—so his head could think despite all the noise. He closed his eyes and pretended he was watering Brandy's garden. Or nuzzling the baby in bed.

He'd made a miracle, and yet he'd chosen to put his ass all the way over here. But he was doing it to help protect someone else's innocent women and children. He hoped that, if the situation were reversed, someone would do the same—protect his wife and baby.

T.J. leaned over, "You okay?"

"I was just thinking—don't get me wrong now."

"Uh oh. Not one of those conversations." T.J. picked up a rock and threw it.

"Kyle told me you held him. Held Frankie."

"T.J. sorted the rubble at his feet, looking for another rock, and then picked up several.

"Yeah, I did."

"And he made you promise."

T.J. nodded.

"You're a good man. And now you're raising Frankie's daughter."

"Yup, I got a little piece of Frankie with me always. And she's my daughter now, Tucker."

"You're right. That's the way it should be, too."

"Yup."

"It must have been hard."

"Frankie wasn't going to make it. I would have promised him anything just to keep him alive. It wasn't going to happen."

Tucker was hesitant to continue. They sat in silence. Then Tucker had to speak. "Would you do the same for me?"

"Hell no."

"Why?" Tucker felt the tiny flame of anger growing inside.

"'Cause I'd go to jail, and I'd never do that to Shannon."

Tucker grinned. He hadn't even thought about Shannon. Of course, he wouldn't take on another wife.

"It's not funny, Tucker. That's a damn serious thing."

Sven was listening, his arms crossed, stifling a

smile.

"I didn't mean *marry* her. What do you take me for? I meant help get her set up. With another Team Guy. Somebody good."

"Listen to you, Tuck. I never expected to hear those words come out of your mouth."

"But would you do it?"

"Well, let me ask you, would you?"

Tucker nodded again. "Yes. Yes, I would."

"Well then, there you have your answer."

The two men clasped hands to the sounds of Sven chuckling in the background.

CHAPTER 16

GERI AND BRYCE arrived an hour later. Keira was thrilled to see them, yanking on Geri's arm to show her the playhouse. She ran inside and out, opened the windows and doors and got Geri to bend down and join her.

Bryce was stiff and, as he'd said over the phone, was not making eye contact with Brandy. But he did look at the baby in her arms and finally said, "She's a cutie. God, I remember those days. Some of the best of my life."

Brandy smiled, but inside, she felt the pain this man was feeling. "They grow up quick, don't they?"

He did return her gaze this time. He had that same look about him as Tucker did, not shying from going to the heart of the problem. He showed no weakness, not even a little weepy-eyed tear. He was on a mission. His handsome face a total mask of what must be churning inside.

"Make the most of every day. None of us know what can happen in the future. And don't assume anything." He cleared his throat and watched his wife and child outside.

"I'm sure there's no way you—"

He interrupted her. "I'm not going there until we find this guy. There's always something we can do." He put his huge hand on top of Kimberly's head with a tenderness that made her knees weak. "Goes to show how one little lapse in attention can cause things to derail." He smiled at Kimberly and then raised his eyes to Brandy. "I had a hunch, and I didn't act on it. That's on me."

Brandy knew better than to argue with him. She felt he was being far too hard on himself. But Tucker would feel the same.

"It's a good lesson for all of us." She saw the police car pull up to the front of the house. "I think your friend is here."

Bryce greeted the uniformed officer at Brandy's front door, as well as the social worker sent from the Department.

"Brandy, this is Kent Porter. He and I go way back to when he tried out for the Teams."

The handsome dark-haired officer extended his hand. "Brandy, just so you know, we don't talk about that much, and if Bryce is lucky, he won't bring it up again."

She liked him and felt reassured by his firm handshake.

"This is Mary Weck. She's one of our social workers we contract when we're interviewing kids. One of the best."

"Nice to meet you, Brandy. Thank you for reporting the incident right away. That gives us some ammunition to go on."

"You're welcome. So how does this work?"

The social worker began. "We'll interview her here, and I think I'll have her mom with her. Bryce, perhaps not you. I think you and Kent should go outside for a bit, go get a coffee or something, but be on hand in case we need you."

"Fine," he said. "Got my cell."

"Brandy, I think it would be good for you to be here as well, because she felt it was safe to tell you about it in the first place. And she will know what she told you, instead of trying to cover it up or deny it. But she may do that anyway."

"Okay. I may have to get up and down with the baby."

"I think that's good. Normal life here. We're in a friend's house. Her parents are here. Less scary than going downtown or in my strange office." She smiled. "Although I do have some pretty nice toys."

Brandy chuckled. "I have some books in the little chest over there, if you need anything like that. I read a couple of them to her earlier today."

"Perfect. Shall we get started, Bryce?"

The two men left in the patrol car.

Brandy went to the back door and motioned for Geri to come inside. Holding hands, they both walked inside. Keira's eyes got wide when she saw the woman sitting on Brandy's couch.

"Keira, this is Mrs. Weck. She's a nice lady who wants to talk to you for a few minutes, okay?"

Keira clutched Geri's skirt like she'd first done when she arrived earlier.

"Here, Mommy will sit next to you, right here, okay?"

The six-year-old climbed into her mother's lap and buried her face in Geri's neck and chest. Her eyes fixated on Brandy, standing to the side, as if she had some idea what this was all about.

"I understand your sister has a boyfriend," Mary began.

Keira's face wrinkled in pain as she shot Brandy a harsh look.

"Can you answer Mrs. Weck?" murmured Geri to the top of her head.

Keira kept her face turned away from the social worker and didn't move.

Mary Weck started again, "Keira, you're not in any trouble, but we wanted to ask you about your sister's boyfriend. What can you tell me about him?"

"I don't know anything," she said into her mother's chest. Brandy could see she'd begun to cry. Geri continued to rub her daughter's back in soothing, long motions.

Mary's voice was patient and slow, but she continued to pry for information. "How do you know she has a boyfriend? Have you seen him?"

"No," she mumbled.

"Keira, we understand you may have seen a picture of him on your sister's cell phone. Is that correct?"

That got her to sit up and face the room. "I didn't see his face, just his pee pee."

Geri's eyes closed, a single tear tracing down her right cheek.

"Thank you for that, Keira. That's very good," said Mary. She refrained from touching the child. "When did you see his picture?"

"I forgot."

"Was it yesterday or the day before?"

"I don't remember."

"How did you see it?"

"He sends her text messages. And he sent her the picture. I saw it before she put the phone away. She asked me if I saw it, and I told her no."

"What else?"

"She made me promise not to tell Mommy and Daddy. Made me keep it our secret." She looked up at her mother. "I didn't want to keep a secret."

"I know, sweetheart," Geri said as she hugged her.

"Don't tell Dad. He'll be really mad."

Mary looked between Geri and her daughter, then said, "Honey, he already knows. And he's not mad at you at all. Your mother's spoken to him."

Keira stared back into Geri's face. "Really?"

"Yes, honey. Nobody's mad."

"Well, Lynn will be. She's going to smash up all my dolls. I know she will."

Mary paused, waiting for her to finish and then spoke softly. "We're here to help Lynn, because we need to find that boyfriend quickly before he sends any more pictures to her, or to anybody else. Do you understand?"

Keira nodded.

"You wouldn't want to get pictures like that, would you?"

"No. They're yucky."

"Yes, they are. And have you ever seen any other pictures? Or has Lynn told you she received others?"

"She didn't tell me. I just saw one."

"Okay, so is this boyfriend someone she's known a long time or just a short time?"

Keira shrugged.

"Someone from school?"

She shrugged again. "He wants to meet her, so I think he goes to another school."

"So, she hasn't met him yet?"

Keira shook her head.

"Now Keira, I'm going to ask you a very important question, and it might be difficult to answer, okay?"

Keira nodded.

"Can you tell me, how did you know it was a picture of his pee pee?"

She frowned, puzzled. "I know what a boy looks like. I've seen my Daddy naked before—by accident."

"How by accident?"

"I've seen him getting dressed, on accident. I didn't mean to!" She stared up at her mother. "I'm sorry."

"It's okay, Keira," said Geri.

"So tell me more about what it looked like," Mary pressed.

"It was pink and fuzzy with hair all over it. It looked disgusting."

Geri gasped for air, and then softened, hugging Keira tightly, but she could not stifle the tears. Mary Weck sat straight and nodded to herself.

"Okay, I think we're done," she said.

CHAPTER 17

TUCKER'S CELL RANG.

"Fredo and the gang are done. You ready to head back?" barked Gibson.

"They picked up the target?"

"They did. We got a lot of information to digest. We'll see you back up here in a few."

"Roger that."

"We done here?" asked T.J.

Tucker spotted his four Teammates exiting the building. "Sven, go tell Fredo to put a mark on that car. I'll meet you back at the Jeep, okay?"

"I'm on it," Sven said as he emerged from the shadows to meet the other squad.

Tucker and T.J. waited until the tracker was placed, counted another five minutes to make sure no one had seen them place the mark, and then carefully emerged from the shadows. Sven was waiting for them at the Jeep.

The sun hung lower in the horizon as a golden bronze covered everything, softening some of the harshness of the bright colors they'd seen earlier on. It also smoothed over the contrast between the lush gardens that popped up on the shore side, behind guarded gates, and the highway and villages where most the population lived. It was like the population was divided into two groups, and it had nothing to do with nationality. There were the working people, families and children, shopkeepers and the rescuers and civil servants trying to help them function in all the chaos. Then there were the other people who worked very hard to separate themselves from that general population.

So what group do I belong to?

He decided he didn't belong in any group. Not above or below, but separate, operating in the shadows and free from the routine of everyday life. At least that's what it was like here. At home, well, in a way, he lived in the shadows too, since so much of what he did for a living was a total secret. They had their own world, and in that world, there was security, family, love, and a future.

"So those two are staying at the hotel, then?" Tucker asked Sven.

"Yes. The guys took some pictures of them checking in and heading upstairs."

"Did they meet up with anyone?" T.J. asked.

"They didn't say."

"So we kinda made Diego think we were coming back tonight, Tuck. We going to do that?"

"Let's wait to see what Gibson says. Maybe we should give one of the other squads a chance."

"I'm game for whatever," added Sven.

The crush of traffic grew more intense until they got through to the other side of Las Palmas, and then a steady stream of gravel trucks and bulldozers on trailers filed past them coming down the hill from the site of the fires. They turned up to finish the stretch to their motel.

A roadblock had been set up where a bus had overturned in front of them. Flares and lights flashed everywhere. It was difficult to see who was directing traffic, so everything just stopped. An ambulance passed them going up the oncoming lane and then a fire truck. Several groups of locals had gathered, watching the mess.

"Geez, hope Fredo got through," said T.J.

"No kidding." Tucker called the house and got Gibson. "We're stuck behind an overturned bus. Should we offer to help?"

"That's a negative, Tucker. We're not to get involved."

So they waited. He turned off the Jeep.

At last, as darkness approached, they were directed to skirt the accident. Tucker had to dodge curious onlookers—even a boy on horseback and half a dozen food carts. Faces of all colors shouted in languages he couldn't understand. Women wrapped in colorful drapes with baskets and children in tow were illuminated by the red and blue flashing lights. The whole scene looked like one of the many carnival parades he'd seen.

Compared to the snarled traffic jam, the rest of the drive home was uneventful.

The house was eating dinner when they arrived. Tucker wanted to get the grit and grime of the day off him but was too starved to wait. An enormous spread had been laid out for them with several local dishes, fresh fruits, and some barbeque chicken, which was heavenly. He stuffed himself.

They were to have an evening briefing, so he ran upstairs to make a quick call to Brandy and perhaps get a quick shower in. He found Sven just getting out.

"I feel human again," he said.

"That's right where I'm headed." As he slipped off his shoes, he asked his Norwegian friend a question. "How much time did you say you spent here? And when was that, Sven?"

"Oh God, twenty, yeah, twenty years ago. Just before I joined the forces."

Tucker had stripped off everything except his shorts. "What brought you here?"

"I did a lot of traveling. We do a lot of that in Europe. Kids used to travel all over the place, all over the world in their teens."

"I've heard that."

"I'd never been to the Canaries. Someone said it had nice beaches."

"We never saw any of that before, did we? Haven't seen any this time, either."

"Nope. Not what we're here for. We've been in the seedier parts, the old harbor. Downtown has wide streets and cathedrals, very different than here. All the islands are different. But, yes, I had a good time."

"So she was an art student. How'd you live? Were you working?"

"Tended a little bar. That's how I met her. And then we had a place on Tenerife. Came here for a weekend. It was a lovely hotel."

"What happened?" Tucker asked.

"Life happened. Her parents demanded she return home. Said they didn't want to finance her Norwegian fling any longer." He laughed. "I think I made her drop out of school."

"I'd have thought you would have inspired her art."

Sven shrugged. "It was what it was."

The shower was heavenly. With fresh clothes, he

flew downstairs and sat just as their meeting was beginning. Then he remembered he'd not called Brandy.

Lt. Commander Gibson began their briefing with, "We're off to a good start, gents. The hairnets are giving Stuart and his team fits. They've got so much information. Stuart told me we're going to have some very specific locations to kick some serious butt coming up here."

Tucker was relieved.

"Fredo's got a trace on a car we hope will help locate some of the players who aren't quite so public. We've identified one of the six names on our list, Javier Rodriguez, who we believe is staying at the Tradewinds. I think Tucker and T.J. and Sven have started something at the Capri, but we've definitely got a tight fix on Rodriguez, and that's huge for our first day out."

"Do we have to worry they'll find the tracking device," asked Coop. "I mean, should we try to mark them in more than one place?"

"That's up to Stuart and the guys back home. Our job is to find all six and bring them in, hopefully at the same time, and get them somewhere we can interrogate them." He paced the floor just as he commonly did back in Coronado. "What else we're following is some ferry activity down at Gondolia Harbor. Not sure if any of you noticed that large cruise ship that some-one pressed into service. It's Italian registry?"

Several men acknowledged seeing it.

"We think there are ferries operating out of port, using this ship to offload or make exchanges. Jens Vandershoot's family is in shipping, and Jens was a known associate of VanValle, the guy you got last mission. This time, we want to capture the asshole and find out about all his locations, all his illegal businesses. We want to put him away so that someone else doesn't crop up later on and take over, like he did."

Gibson described several of the other characters on their list of most wanted. And he stressed that someone was going to have to make it onto that cruise ship somehow.

"Do we have equipment for that? Rebreathers?" asked T.J.

"We do. It's about a five-mile swim from where we can launch a team. We need some eyes on that ship from the inside. We've watched containers being off-loaded, but they're putting some back on, too. We need to verify what they've got."

Gibson brainstormed some of the intelligence theo-ries and asked for four men to show up at Diego's night club pretending to look for girls. Tucker was relieved when he chose Lucas, Alex, Jake, and Ryan, who were all long-time friends, for that mission.

"The rest of you, hang out a bit and turn in early. Tomorrow will be a long day. And I'll need one squad awake in case Lucas and the others get into trouble. We'll have our targets, as well as the required permissions, in the morning."

Tucker ran upstairs to try to get a call in to Brandy. He replayed her message back first and was alarmed to hear she was having difficulty. Checking the time, he figured she'd be awake and placed the call but didn't get an answer.

"Hey, Brandy. Just trying to reach you. Got me a little concerned. Call me when you get this. Don't worry about what time it is here. Wanna talk to you."

He straightened his things, located his journal, and began to write like he'd promised.

I'm kind of glad I'm not seeing the best part of the island. Sven told me he'd spent some time here with a Spanish girl twenty years ago. Talked about the beaches and the great hangouts on one of the other islands. Maybe someday we could do a "just vacation" trip over here, although avoiding anywhere I've been this time.

The buildings are like little pill boxes piled up on top of each other, colors of red, light blue, white, and bright yellow. They like their colors, similar to the Caribbean. It's a little more prosperous than Africa. More Spanish influence, which is why there are cathedrals everywhere.

We're over in a more remote portion of the island than we were before. More industrial. And, with all the international aid going on right now, it's so congested and noisy I can't hear myself think. That and the heat. Good news is, no bugs so far! And I haven't seen a snake yet, either.

Got to taste some Boss Beer, which is like it sounds—beer made by the "boss." Using corn, not wheat, barley, or hops. Can't say I'm a fan yet. But bottled beer and water are safest when you don't know where it's coming from.

Hope those palm trees are doing well. I miss everything about home, but mostly, I miss you, Brandy.

He folded up his notebook and lay back on the bed.

THE PHONE RANG and pulled him out of a deep sleep. Sven was snoring and apparently didn't hear a thing.

"Brandy?" Tucker checked his watch, and it was not quite 0300.

"So glad I could talk to you. I really needed to hear your voice."

"Your message—"

"I shouldn't have bothered you with it. That was me at a weak moment. Last thing you want to do is worry about things over here."

"So what's up?" he whispered. Sven stirred in his bed but didn't awake.

"This situation with Lynn Tanner. Today we had an interview with her little sister, and it looks like there's an older guy, perhaps a man, involved."

"Lynn's involved with an older man?" Tucker walked downstairs so he could speak without being overheard. "What are they doing?"

"So much has happened, and I don't want to bother you with it."

"Tell me. I'll stay up all night if I have to, Brandy."

"They interviewed Keira last night, at the house. They confirmed what Keira had told me and discovered that this person sending Lynn messages is probably an older man. Or, at least, not a child. Now they're looking for a sexual predator, that it wasn't just a kid's type of prank. Somehow this guy has gotten hold of her cell phone and convinced her he's a teenager."

"Bryce must be beside himself." Tucker's guts were in knots. He knew the waiting was the worst part of any emergency. His mind was filling with worry. "Brandy, listen to me. Maybe you should go over to Dorie's house or have someone come there to be with you. Get your dad to come or take Kimberly there."

"That's a good idea. But Kimberly is too young to

take to someone else's place. Joe Benson and his friends were here all afternoon building Kimberly a beautiful little pink playhouse. You should see it, Tucker. Keira was so excited for her."

"Call Joe, Brandy. Call Joe and Gloria. You don't have to tell them everything, but it's important that you don't stay home by yourself. You'll be peeking out every window and making up things you might see. Will you do that, honey?"

"I should have thought about that. I feel so stupid. I hardly slept last night."

"You have to learn to reach out. I can't be there all the time, sweetie. I just can't. This is part of why it's hard, being a SEAL wife is hard. But you don't have to be alone and afraid. Being strong is asking for help."

"You're right, Tucker. I'm beating myself up now for not being tougher."

"And that's wrong too. This is all new for you. It's new to me, too."

He wasn't going to mention it was why SEAL marriages often failed. There was such a disconnect when they were away. Not everyone was cut out to handle it. He blamed some of that on the failure of his first marriage. Being scared to be alone made finding someone else an attractive option. It was the option Shayla took. Still, he knew Brandy would never do that. He'd have to pay more attention to things when he got home.

"Brandy, I'm going to say something that might sound harsh. Please just listen, okay?"

"Okay."

"You have to separate yourself from the rest of the crazy world. You have to build a wall around every awful thing that could happen when I'm away. You can't fix everything, help everybody. Terrible things happen within our own community. It's just life. And, as awful as this sounds, it has nothing to do with us. You've got to understand that. Let other people handle it the way they need to. You need to detach and try not to get involved."

"But that feels so cruel."

"You'll go crazy, Brandy. And I can't come home and fix everything all the time." He didn't want to go further, but it was time she understood some of the stakes.

"You have to ask yourself what you'd do if I didn't come home. What if it was like Frankie?"

"Don't say that, Tucker!"

"Sweetheart, I'm telling you this because that's always a possibility. It isn't all roses and glitter all the time. You have to be real."

"I don't want to think about that. Ever."

"You have to, Brandy. Your job is to take care of Kimberly. That's your only job. Everything else in the world can just go flush itself, for all I care. You have to be there for her."

He knew he'd made her cry. He was beginning to get angry with himself. He should have tempered his tone.

Dammit.

This is so fuckin' hard.

"Are you still there, sweetheart?"

He heard her sigh. "Yes."

"I get trained to do these crazy things. We learn how to tap down our emotions, even when they're raging inside us. Do you know why they teach us that?"

"So you stay alert."

"That's right. Because why we're worrying about one thing, something else pops up. The only difference between what I do and what you do is that you're a team of one when I'm gone. You are Kimberly's whole world. Am I making any sense, 'cause I'll keep talking until I do. I've got all the time in the world."

"But you won't get any sleep."

"Hell, I know what going without sleep is all about. That's not a problem." His heart lurched, and he dug his fingers into his palm, making a fist until it hurt and began to bleed. She was more of a rock to him than she realized. He wasn't sure he'd gotten through.

And then a miracle happened.

"Thank you, Tucker."

Her voice got soft. The tightness in her throat was gone from holding back tears.

"I think I understand now. I needed to hear that. You're exactly right. I was taking my eye off the ball for a while. I was overwhelmed."

"It's okay."

"But that part about you not coming back. I'll never forgive you if you do that."

They both laughed. He was laughing through his tears but controlled his breath so she wouldn't know.

"That's my girl. You see, the one part I didn't tell you was that I depend on you as much as you depend on me. I understand what you're going through because I *want* to understand you. You're my rock, baby. Yours is the face I come home to, see every night. Everything I see that's good in the world reminds me of you. All I need is for you to be strong for me. Just a few more days. And I'll be home, and we can celebrate."

She sniffled, and he knew she was a snotty mess, which gave him a chuckle inside.

"That will be a great day, Tucker. Can't wait."

"The whole world can go to Hell, and we're still gonna be here. It's you and me, Brandy. I see stuff every day in these places that's just fucked up. It just shouldn't be that way. Women and kids abused, innocents caught up in something they didn't create.

They just want to have the kind of life we can have. I learned long ago that I can't fix everything. I can only do my part."

"You come home, Tucker. I want you to teach me how to be brave. Neither one of us knows what's in store for either of us. I want you to teach me to prepare for anything."

"You got it, babe. It will be my pleasure."

After they signed off, Tucker waited until the vibration he felt all over his body stopped. That familiar engine that was running inside, all the rage he felt at all the things that were wrong with the world would never leave him. It was part of who he was.

And it always would be his job to do whatever he could. He just couldn't live any other way. He would never quit. Not while there was work to be done.

It was what coming home was all about—to see his family live in the safety he'd helped to create. To enjoy the twinkle in their eyes and the freedom in their hearts.

CHAPTER 18

S TEPHEN COOK CAME right over with his new wife, Jillian. He brought several bags of fresh produce with them, and after taking turns with Kimberly, the two of them took up their stations in the kitchen peeling, chopping, and making heavenly smells. Brandy was so happy she'd called him.

She asked if they could have Joe and Gloria Benson over for dinner as well, and so, the five of them sat down upstairs on the plywood tabletop, decorated with votive candles, drinking wine and serving up the feast.

"Joe's still talking about all the projects he wants to do here," beamed Gloria.

"Steven, you're welcome to come on over, if you're handy. We just need the okay from the boss, here," Joe Benson said, pointing to Brandy.

"We're on a rather precarious budget at the time, Joe. But—"

"Hogwash," said Joe.

"Not a problem," said her father.

The two older women rolled their eyes and helped themselves to more wine.

"Whatever do you mean, Dad?" Brandy asked him.

"Well, whatever he needs, I can buy. He's donating the labor. I guess I could donate the cost of construction."

"You don't have to do that," she answered him.

"Of course he does." Jillian toasted her.

Joe retrieved some plans he'd started to draw up. "These are only preliminary, of course. And, before we dig in here, first priority is to get that backyard fenced and gated. Agreed?"

"I agree," she said.

"So here we are." He rolled out drawings done on tracing paper. "You can see how we can add this second bathroom downstairs, move the walls a bit and create a nice master bedroom closet?"

"Looks like we'd have two bedrooms and two baths then. Is that right?"

"You got it." Joe continued to demonstrate the changes to the downstairs while Jillian and Gloria cleared off the table and took everything into the kitchen.

Brandy leaned in on her elbows and studied the plans. "So you'd have the entrance for the upstairs here," she pointed out. "That would be right about there, by that big window."

"No, that would be the doorway. We take the window out and make it a doorframe instead. We also make a deck just big enough for a small table and chairs. Great place to watch sunsets." Joe angled for agreement from Steven Cook.

"I like it. But boy, I'd have a hard time deciding which unit to live in. Pretty nice up here," Cook said.

Brandy agreed. "I know. I love sewing and laying out projects here. The light is wonderful. Makes me want to start painting again."

"You should. Joe, she's really talented."

"Well, this could be your studio. Maybe find a couple other artists to share the space with. Who knows, maybe you could rent it out that way."

"It's a thought. Not sure the zoning would allow a commercial space. But we know for sure we can do a second unit. The city is trying to encourage more housing. I know we could use the extra income."

She hesitated to bring up the subject again.

"Just how much is this going to cost? I mean, I don't want you guys to do all of this for free."

"If I don't have to pay for materials, I absolutely don't mind doing the labor. You will have to get a plumber and electrician, and I know the permits will cost you something. A few thousand dollars." Joe shrugged, "But we'll know more after my friend Sy does the structural engineering. You're going to need all that to put in for your permit. I'll get an idea what Sy will charge, but we're all retired. We actually look for projects like this we can do together just to stay active. We built a big play structure over at the church a month ago."

"You like the ideas, Brandy?" her dad asked.

She thought about the conversation she'd had with Tucker earlier this morning. "I can't wait. I think Tucker would be pleased. I'm going to tell him first chance we get to talk."

The men sat back in their chairs.

"How's he doing?" Joe asked.

"I guess he and T.J. went on a little trip yesterday. He said it was very chaotic, with all the cleanup and evacuations happening."

"What's he doing, exactly?" her dad wanted to know.

"Beat's me," she shrugged. "Like all of them, it's just a mission. Something to do with bad guys doing evil things. Same old, same old."

Joe chuckled. "Frankie's mother went nuts every time he went over, before he got married. Of course, he didn't call us, like he probably does now, but he never would tell us anything. Said he was on the beach, chasing girls. His mom would get so frustrated with him."

Brandy's dad gave Joe a warm smile. "You've got a granddaughter, right?"

"Love of my life!" said Joe.

"Who's the love of your life?" shouted Gloria Benson. She had a pie in one hand and a carafe of coffee in the other.

"I was talking about our Courtney."

"Look who's up," said Jillian, holding Kimberly. "I changed her for you. Hope that was okay."

"Oh my, thank you."

Kimberly's eyes were trying to focus on the candlelight. Her little head jerked from side to side as she tried to hold herself up.

"Look how strong she is already. That's amazing," said Gloria.

As the baby nursed, Brandy was suddenly grateful for the older people in her life, sharing her young joy with their years of experience. Her father had found love again after the passing of her mother. Joe and Gloria lived through Courtney, their son's child.

She did feel safe. Tucker had been right. Her job was to make sure she wasn't alone, to make sure to stay plugged in and connected with her family and her community.

After Joe and Gloria Benson left, Brandy's dad and Jillian were preparing for bed.

"You never did tell me why you wanted us to come

over," her dad said. He was always the one who observed her many moods growing up.

"I told you. It was about time we spent more time together. I don't want to take her out too much until she's older." She checked his expression to see if he was buying the lie. "I was getting lonely, I guess. Stir crazy."

"Has something happened? Did you see something on the news?"

"I don't watch the news much. I don't want to see something about a conflict in Africa or someplace where Tucker might be." She pulled the baby up on her shoulder and burped her. She considered whether or not she should tell her father about Keira and Lynn and decided to wait until she knew more what the outcome was. She remembered what Tucker had said, *Let the experts handle it. Nothing you can do.* "Thanks for being concerned. I'm fine now. Seeing all you guys tonight was exactly what I needed."

"Well, I'm off to bed. We'll make breakfast in the morning. Then we can discuss how long you want us to stay."

"Thanks, Dad," she said as she stood. They walked down the hallway to the bedrooms. Steven Cook kissed his granddaughter and then kissed his daughter.

"Love you, Brandy. Your mom would be so happy to see you and the baby. I'm glad you're so happy."

If he only knew.

CHAPTER 19

L T. COMMANDER GIBSON shook Tucker awake. At first, he couldn't remember where he was, but then Sven's familiar snoring brought him right back.

"We got a problem. One of the boys got arrested," Gibson said.

"Shit." He was putting on his jeans and a shirt. "Who is it?"

"Lucas Shipley."

"Stupid fuck. How did that happen?"

"Alex thinks it's a shakedown. They're staying down there at the police station until we can figure something out."

"You call State?"

Gibson hesitated. "They want to see if we can get him out first. Try paying them off, and that's what they think has to happen. But they'll contact the folks in Madrid if that doesn't work."

"I'd like to take T.J. then unless—"

"I'm good with that. You know where the station is?"

"No, but I'll find out. I need Alex's cell. I'll wanna talk to him on the way down."

Gibson shared the contact. "I'll go get T.J."

"I understand my presence is requested," he said, carrying all his clothes.

They checked in with Stuart Bonilla, who was fast asleep on a mattress in the corner of the communications room. One of his men sat at the console, removing his headset.

"Hola!"

"We've got to go get a man at the police station. Anything I should know about?"

Stuart jumped up off the mattress. "Sorry, I've been up for nearly twenty-four hours. I was seeing things."

"We're going back into Las Palmas to pick up Lucas, who's gotten arrested. Anything big going on that you know of?"

"No. I got no clusters. Nothing's moving. Right, Ray?" he asked the young agent at the desk.

"I got nothing. Lots of things I'm looking for in the morning, but all's quiet now."

"Tucker, check in so we know you got successfully home."

"Will do. You want me to take the net?"

"Let's leave that home, just in case you get

searched. Say, Gibson," Stuart addressed the Lt. Commander, "who had the device?"

"I gave it to Jake. I know it wasn't Lucas."

"Okay, good. Those fuckers are expensive."

"Stuart," said the young agent. "They turned it off over an hour ago. I got nothing on it, just the bartender's signal and he wasn't making calls."

"Okay, we're on our way."

Tucker and T.J. started up the Jeep and used the glow from a nearly full moon to navigate the winding road down the hill.

He called Alex.

"We're on our way. Can you tell me what happened?"

"It was just a crazy bar scene. A couple of locals found out we were Americans and started messing with us. The bartender tried to make them leave, but they started a fight."

"How come they nabbed Lucas? How did that happen?"

The dead space on the other end of the line said volumes. "Lucas punched them back."

"That was smart."

"One of them has a brother who is a Civil Guard. Real mean dude. There wasn't anything we could say. I don't think they're going to hurt him, just keep him there overnight."

"And you think this how?"

"That's what the bartender told us. He told us to go home and not to worry about him."

"You think the bartender knows these guards?"

"I think everyone knows everyone. He just didn't want to have trouble. He'd brought some ladies for us to dance with, you know. We weren't going to do anything, just buy them some drinks and such. Then these guys got jealous. Had a chip on their shoulder about Americans."

"How close to the Capri is the station?"

"About five, six blocks. I'll drive to the Capri, and you can follow us over."

"Good. See you in a few."

They didn't pass a single vehicle until they got to the bottom and hit the outskirts of the city. The harbor was fully lit up, and as they passed by, they saw forklifts stacking small containers while a crane was loading a shipping car into the large cargo opening on the cruise ship. A platform had been attached to the outside to facilitate the transfer of goods. Men with lighted hard hats guided the container until it was swallowed in the belly of the ship.

"They're working late," Tucker commented.

"I was just noticing that. Wonder what they're loading."

"I guess we'll find out soon."

The temporary buildings were well lit, but it appeared most everyone was asleep. Several fenced off areas were patrolled by Civil Guards with dogs.

The Capri was closed, but Tucker found Jake, Alex, and Ryan in the shadows, along the side that lead to the Tradewinds. Tucker noticed the car that Fredo had tagged was still there.

Tucker rolled down his window. "Anyone notice you?"

"We haven't attracted anyone's attention that we know of."

"Where are the guys who picked a fight?"

"Gone. They were gone by the time the police showed up."

"Okay, lead the way, then."

He followed the dirty sedan with the rubbed-out paint, noticing that it also smoked like hell. They turned several times and then came to a small plaza with a fountain in the middle. The streets were paved in cobblestone, so the ride made Tucker's teeth chatter. On one end of the plaza stood a two-story building with a flat, tiled roof, and small windows. Tucker knew it was the local jail.

Two blue and white compact patrol cars and one scooter were parked outside. He asked Alex and T.J to come with him, and the three of them mounted the steps, finding themselves inside a tiled foyer. A blue-uniformed Civil Guard stood and immediately approached them with a stick of some kind. Tucker thought he was going to be struck.

The official said something in Spanish, and Tucker put his hands out to the side. "Americans. We're Americans. You have our friend inside," He pointed to somewhere beyond the wall.

"I scan," the guard said and waved a wand down Tucker's front and back sides, repeating it with all three.

"No weapons. No problem," T.J. said.

Tucker gave a scowl but then turned to discuss Lucas' situation. "You speak English, senior?"

"Little."

"We come to pay his fine," Tucker said.

"Fine? What is fine?"

"Money. We are sorry, my friend. He's my brother. He marry my sister. My sister be very angry if I don't bring him home."

"He marry your sister?"

"Yes, tomorrow. Ceremony tomorrow."

"No, Senior. Not possible."

"My sister, she loves this man. She will be very, very angry. She knows many rich people."

Tucker wasn't sure the guard was very interested in helping them. There was no way they should break Lucas out, although he knew they could pull it off. It was exactly the thing that they'd been told not to do. Then he had an idea.

"You can call my sister's boss, Jens Vandershoot. Call him. He will vouch for my friend."

The guard eliminated his slouch and practically stood to attention. "You know Jens Vandershoot?"

Tucker could see panic in the man's face.

"Old family friend. Go ahead, call him. But it's very early. Perhaps we pay the fine and take him home now, so he doesn't miss the wedding, okay?"

Tucker reached into his jacket pocket and brought out a stack of one hundred U.S. dollar bills, with its red sticker still attached. He held the stack up to the guard's face. "Brand new. Virgin bills. For my friend."

The guard indicated he'd be right back and left, without taking the money.

"Well, I've either fucked all of us up or made a dent in the problem."

T.J. chuckled. "We should have brought DeWayne. He could have talked to this guy no problem."

"Well, I was going for authenticity."

"You were that, Tucker," added Alex.

The door the guard exited into opened, and Lucas was pushed out in front of them. He had a swollen eye and dried blood from a cut lip. The guard unlocked his handcuffs and applied a damp towel to Lucas' face.

"Tomorrow, he will be perfect, see?" He dabbed the

blood and pressed lightly on Lucas' eye. Lucas grabbed the towel and growled.

"Thank you, my friend," Tucker said bowing, presenting the stack of bills. When the guard took it, Tucker added, "And I will be sure to tell Mr. Vandershoot how cooperative you were."

The guard's eyes got wide. He started to push the money back. "No, no. There is no problem. It is my pleasure."

Lucas took the money back and started to stuff it back in his jacket but stopped. "Ah, hell, you earned it. Thank you, and I won't say anything to Mr. Vandershoot."

The guard held the bills with both hands, like they were a bouquet of flowers.

"You are most kind."

As they were leaving the lobby, Lucas asked. "Where did you get the cash?"

"Gibson gave it to me. But, Lucas, why did you think it was a good idea to punch the guy?'

"He said the Cubs sucked."

CHAPTER 20

B RANDY'S DAD INSISTED that either he or Jillian would spend the nights with Brandy until Tucker came home. She'd get more sleep, and they could help with the housework and the cooking. Jillian coordinated with some of the wives and tapered off the fried chicken and heavy foods. Each time, Kimberly was paraded out for all to see. Everyone offered support. Brandy saw that she'd not been taking full advantage of the help offered before, while she had it.

She also knew that this wouldn't last forever.

Geri gave her updates over the next few days. Despite the questioning Lynn had undergone, the person who had stalked her and her cell phone had completely vanished. The pictures were turned over to the police, but it was determined that not much else could be done. No one was sure how this person had obtained Lynn's phone number in the first place, but they suspected it was someone local when she'd ordered fast food or put her name down for a newsletter at a shop of some kind. The police continued to think it was a random occurrence and wasn't likely to reoccur.

Lynn's high school presented a program on human smuggling and sex trafficking for parents, as the result of what her family had gone through. But Lynn's anonymity was kept intact, and, except for her family and the school staff, what she'd gone through wasn't common knowledge. The social worker, police, and her counselor at school all told her how lucky she had been, and Lynn seemed to accept it and agree with them.

Steve enjoyed working in the garden, sometimes with Brandy, and kept the rows neatly tended. He helped Joe Benson and his two buddies work on the side gate and rear fence until it was completed. Sy had turned plans into the City to be approved for the addition, with Brandy's dad paying the permit fees, which amounted to nearly a thousand dollars. They were given a two-month window for everything to be processed. Of course, nothing would start until Tucker came home to approve everything. But it was all ready to go, just in case.

Dorie stopped by with her three. The twins were nearly walking. Jessica was very curious of the baby, but once she saw the playhouse in back, she refused to come inside and stayed until dark. She spent the whole afternoon presenting the men with imaginary tea and sandwiches from her playhouse.

"I think Joe's going to have a steady stream of orders for those," said Dorie. "You think he's ready for that?"

"Hope so. I'm so happy they've still got a home with all of us. It must be terrible to lose a son like he did."

"Brawley said one of the instructors told him about a man they lost a few years ago, who left behind a wife and two kids. The team nearly came to fistfights over the widow."

"No!"

"Oh, they're serious about that, Brandy. I mean, I know Brawley would want another Team guy to raise our brood if something happened to him. That's just how it's done."

"I know. Tucker tried to talk to me about that one time. I didn't like hearing it then, and I don't like it now."

"We just live for today and trust that tomorrow will be there too. I always keep a part of me in check, though."

"I've had the same thought, Dorie." Brandy put her arm around her friend's shoulder. "You guys seem happy now."

"We are. I didn't know I married such an asshole!"

Brandy laughed.

"He loves giving those BUD/S guys hell. I think it satisfies something inside him. Besides, he says, he's making them stronger for what they have to endure coming up. Not all his instructors saw combat when he was training. Now, all these guys have seen it multiple times. We're preparing a better team for the future."

"I didn't realize that would make a difference, but I can see it does."

"I've heard some of the older SEALs, who never really saw combat, talk about it. They look up to the younger ones. Have a whole lot of respect for what they had to do over in the Middle East."

"I never knew that."

"So when do they come home?" Dorie asked.

"I'm not sure. This one is very different."

"*All* of Kyle's missions are. Man, have they had some unusual assignments. You know they had a cruise ship taken over by terrorists some years back? It was supposed to be a vacation!"

"That was before Tucker re-upped."

"Yeah, Brawley missed it too. But it was something. Christy got a piece of luggage returned from that cruise a couple of weeks ago. That was, what, seven or more years ago? They finally found her luggage."

They both laughed.

"With Kyle gone this time, I'll bet Tucker is taking

a leadership role."

"Yes, I think so." She sighed. "I'll just be glad when they return. We'll have to get together."

"We need to do that. Just think, Kimberly and my twins will be so close in age. I can't wait to plan those parties!"

Brandy was curious about something. "Dorie, I know I talked to you before about being a SEAL wife, but did it change once Jessica was born? I mean, you were engaged when he was going over, but after you had the baby, did you feel—"

"More alone?"

"Is that what I'm saying?" Brandy scratched her head. "Yeah, I guess that's it."

"You're taking care of someone nearly 24/7, and there's no end to the job. Plus, you worry all the time. My mom isn't especially the motherly type, with all her social stuff and her boyfriends, and Brawley's parents live way up on Oregon—well, I didn't have them either. I had you, though, and that was a Godsend."

She hugged Brandy.

"I am lucky with my dad and Joe and everyone. I really am."

"I'm glad you appreciate it. Some couples just don't have that support system. You have to create your own, when it's not there. Not to bring up the past, but I think that's what happened to Tucker's ex. She was afraid of being alone. It wasn't fair, because he was doing all he could. But she couldn't handle it."

Talk of Shayla still stuck like a thorn in her side.

Brandy shook her head. "Nope. I think she was just flawed. Man, she missed out on one of the best men in the whole world. You remember when we had that little encounter. I thanked her for releasing him."

"Oh gosh, I forgot. That was so funny."

Brandy unloaded the dishwasher while they continued.

"I don't miss the not worrying, Brandy. I won't lie to you. That was going to make me very old very quickly. Brawley had all that trouble; I just didn't know who was going to be the man who came home to me. Do you understand?"

"I do."

Dorie gazed out the window at the men who had started to pick up their tools. "It's good for your dad too, Brandy. He needs friends. Lived all those years without your mom, now with a new wife. A man needs man friends. Just something about them wanting to put things together or solve problems or go do crazy stuff. They have to go out and be men. Brawley is so much happier working with those other instructors, being looked up to by the tadpoles."

"And he'll get his twenty."

"Yes, ma'am. We've got a year to figure out what he

does next. It's going to be hard finding something that satisfies outside this group."

Brandy could see Dorie was more worried about it than she let on.

What would Tucker do some day?

CHAPTER 21

T HE PLATOON WAITED an extra day to track and locate as many of their intended targets as they could find. So far, there had been no trace of Jens Vandershoot, but their intel picked up chatter that he was planning to deliver a large shipment of guns— running them down the western coast of Africa, probably to Nigeria. Vandershoot was known to have extensive ties to government entities there that provided cover for his operations. The Special Agents in charge were betting he'd be using the cruise ship. It was said he never liked to be far from his cargo, so, although they'd not located him electronically, they were certain he'd be on the ship.

They hired a deep-sea fishing charter and used it for staging the three-mile dive Coop, Trace, and Tyler would make. The charter's size and weight put them in a class where they could operate at night without a pilot, which would have created too many questions and dashed the element of surprise.

Tucker, Sven, T.J., and Ryan were to drive down to the harbor and board the ship from land. This time, they were armed with their choice of firepower. Tucker chose the SIG Sauer with two extra magazines.

The rest of the team would split to search targets Stuart had identified. All five of the other targets were located within the past twelve hours on land, near the area of the Capri and Tradewinds. Several were staying in residences nearby.

The squads used the cover of darkness, leaving the compound just after midnight. They only had one chance to make the raid, grabbing as many of the six targets as they could. Vandershoot was the prime target.

As their caravan approached the outskirts of Las Palmas, Tucker's and Fredo's groups headed south along the coast. Coop and the divers drove straight through the city to rendezvous with the fishing charter to get closer to the cruise ship via sea.

Tucker parked his Jeep in an alley across the main commercial harbor drive, leaving Ryan with the vehicle to coordinate with Stuart and Gibson at the hotel. Fredo, Armando and others had split off and headed back to the Tradewinds Hotel where two of their targets had been located. They would also explore the neighborhoods nearby for the remainder.

As planned, Sven cut the chain link fencing to gain entry, avoiding the guard station, and snuck along the dimly lit pier. Although some forklift operators were stacking pallets nearby, they were focused on their work. Tucker figured they'd wait for morning to start loading. The cargo bays had been left open, however, and the gangway was chained off, but not guarded.

Inside the ship, they spotted two armed guards sitting behind a desk.

With no one guarding the gangway's lower entrance, it was easy to climb the crisscross structure and wait just under the cargo hold opening.

"We're ready to board," Tucker whispered into his Invisio.

"Copy that," Ryan answered. A few seconds later, Tucker heard, "That's a go, Tucker. God speed."

Sven tapped on the side of the opening with his KA-BAR, which provoked the desired inquiry from one of the guards. As he peered over, Sven pulled him out, twisted his neck, yanked his upper back, and dropped him into the bay. At the same time, Tucker climbed up the other side of the gangway and tackled the distracted second guard, disabling him quickly but leaving him for Sven and T.J. to immobilize. He scampered into the crew hallway, searching both directions and found the area completely clear.

He signaled for Sven and T.J. to join him.

Staying to the outside stairwells, they climbed three floors until they reached the galley doors, which were chained shut. Sven's compact bolt cutters made fast work severing the lock, which gained them access to the kitchen. The entire galley was completely empty. Even the washers and garbage incinerators were idle.

They moved between stainless steel rows of food preparation stations and ovens then through a small crew lounge and out into one of the main restaurants and beyond to the lobby area. The fancy décor and the piped-in music was surreal. But instead of scores of housekeeping staff polishing the floors and wiping down the surfaces, the floors were littered with dirt, paper, half-filled crates, and broken bottles. Leftover trays of food and empty wine glasses were thrown on the floors.

They'd been given a diagram of the ship but also found one posted on the wall by the elevators. They were looking for the Penthouse Suite area, mid hip, floor 11. Amazingly, the elevators had not been disabled.

"We're on deck 11," Tucker informed Stuart.

"Roger that, Tucker. Still a go. Let us know when you identify the Dutchman."

There were four Penthouse suites on this level, two on each side. They agreed to do two at a time on each side, and if their target wasn't on this floor, they would continue going down each floor until they found him.

On the count of three, he and Sven used their small breaching charge, which was relatively quiet. Both rooms they opened were vacant. Down the hall, a door opened, and two young girls poked their heads out, clutching their nightgowns. Tucker put his finger to his lips, and they disappeared quietly.

Running to the other side, they did the same to the next two Penthouse doors, popping the locks simultaneously. This time, they hit gold.

The African warlord, General Two Fingers, sat up, staring into the barrel of Tucker's SIG. Two young girls with him scrambled to the other side of the bed and covered themselves, whimpering.

"You are so awesomely dead, my man," the General growled.

Tucker knew he was staring into the face of pure evil. "And you're going to jail, my man, for a long, long time."

Vandershoot, on the other hand, wore a flannel sleeping gown and socks and had been sleeping alone. He stared back at Sven in disbelief. T.J. secured both men in zip ties behind their backs while Sven gagged and hooded them.

"We have the General and the Dutchman," reported Tucker.

"Roger that. Great work."

They were escorted down the hallway like the scumbags they were. Doors popped open, young girls of several nationalities stepped outside to watch. As Vandershoot passed by one of them, she spat on him.

T.J. followed behind to watch for an armed attempt to foil the capture, but with the end of the barrel pointed to the General's temple, the few guards—who appeared to be private security and not regular Civil Guard—did nothing and dropped their weapons.

As the foursome left, using the gangway, a small crowd of dockworkers had gathered, without any armed militia. Just before they reached the Jeep, they heard the sound of several hull breaches being detonated.

Cooper's team had managed to make sure that ship and all its cargo would not be sailing for parts unknown without spending some considerable time in dry dock. It would remain in the shallow water until inventory and investigation could be completed.

Fredo and the boys who went into town had secured three of the four remaining targets, all without incident. Within an hour, all five men were delivered to the fishing charter. The dive team was loaded, and they all watched as the charter set out in the early morning fog to their rendezvous with the Stennis carrier group, for questioning. Seconds later, the four vehicles were back on the narrow road to the complex.

Other than the two guards on the cruise ship, no one was seriously injured. On the SEAL Team, only Lucas would be returning with a black eye.

It wasn't even daybreak when they returned to the hotel, where congratulations were in order. Lt. Commander Gibson was coordinating with a Spanish Civil Guard patrol to search the ship and seize the contraband. Their arrangement with the Spanish government had been kept to the letter. Now it would be up to the Spanish courts and their jurisdictional departments to bring charges for the corruption and bribery of the local police and to dispose of the contraband.

For now, they'd put a dent into Vandershoot's operation. It was hoped that with the interrogations, more arrests would follow and the smuggling operation would be seriously hampered.

Tucker knew better than to think they'd done anything permanent to the ring. But it was a start, and with the evidence they'd amassed both in person and with surveillance, it was unlikely that any of the men they captured would ever see their way outside of a jail cell.

He also knew that with enough money and power, anyone could ultimately get away. But they'd made it harder for the ring to function and perhaps given some of the families impacted time to take a breath and heal from the violence.

There was no celebration at the end of most their operations. Everyone just wanted to get home, so Gibson ordered them to retire and get some sleep in preparation for the long days of travel ahead.

WHEN TUCKER AWOKE, it was too early for him to let Brandy know they'd be coming home. They'd be stopping over in Virginia for debriefing, expected to take a day plus, and then, possibly be home in San Diego the day after, depending on the transport situation, he'd been told. Anxious to hear her voice, he dialed her anyway.

Her grogginess was such a welcomed sound.

"Tucker, what time is it?"

"Too early but wanted to let you know I'll be home in about three days. We're just wrapping up here."

"Wonderful."

"Now go back to sleep."

"No, I want to talk to you. I can sleep anytime."

He began to unthaw, just hearing her voice. He felt like he was home already.

"How are my two princesses?"

"Your daughter eats like a horse!"

"I would expect nothing less. Is she walking and talking yet?"

Brandy laughed. "Practically. All those nice twelve-month sleepers and tee shirts we got as gifts at the shower, she's nearly grown out of all of them. We're talking eighteen-month, Tucker. She's only a month old!"

"What can I say?"

"I've been spending a lot of time with Dad and Jillian. Thank you for that suggestion. And Joe's been over nearly every day. We have a new back fence and gate at the side of the house. And you should see the garden. You'll be impressed."

"Can't wait. How are you, sweetheart?"

"I haven't lost any weight. The ladies on your team have been forcing food on me. I'm going to have to stop it or I'll look the same as I did pregnant. Jillian has made some wonderful salads. Oh, and I have a surprise for you!"

"Tell me."

"Then it won't be a surprise."

He loved teasing her. He planned to do a lot more of that in the coming weeks.

"Give me a hint, Brandy."

"Nope. You'll have to just keep guessing until I can show you. It has to do with the house, but that's all I can say. I hope you like it."

"We didn't go out and spend a bunch of money, I hope. Did we, Brandy? Remember, our finances are spotty, at best."

"No. Not that."

"You found more palm trees."

"Of course not."

"I give up. Tell me."

"Joe and his buddies have drawn up plans for an addition to our place. Making the second floor another unit. We could Airbnb it or rent it out or make it a studio. We just need your approval to go forward, Tucker."

He was instantly concerned about where the money was going to come from to complete this major project. But he didn't want to dash her hopes. It was just fun to hear the laughter in her voice, the way she enjoyed being a mother.

He couldn't wait to get home.

CHAPTER 22

BRANDY WAS THRILLED to report to her father that Tucker was coming home. She and Jillian cleaned the house while her dad did some last-minute gardening. Some of the furrows needed to be deepened, and since they'd been spending so much time in the rear yard, weeds had cropped up.

The two palm trees were standing as tall as they could, although less than four feet tall. Her dad let her know that the shallow roots had taken hold and were expanding outward, a sure sign they were healthy.

Brandy loved to watch her dad tend to her garden. "You should get one out at the ocean, Dad."

"I think I'd grow some killer artichokes, but I'd have to remove the firepit and the patio. I just couldn't do that to Jillian."

"I get you."

"That's one of the favorite things we do these days, sit back with a nice glass of wine and watch the sunset."

She hugged him from behind. "Happy for you both, Dad."

"I tell you what, though, just this little patch of yard is quite a bit to take care of. You've seen how much work it is."

She nodded. "It's more beautiful than I ever thought possible."

"Wait until the flowers bloom. You'll have mums until Christmas. Then next year, we'll get an early start and get you some real flowers. We'll get a climbing rose for your little fence here—maybe set up a trellis in front of the front door."

"That sounds lovely. I can't wait."

"The snaps we've started will be huge, so you'll have an outstanding spring. I plan on planting some bulbs, if you approve."

"Daffodils. Tucker's favorite flower."

"Ah, that was your mother's as well." He leaned on his shovel. "I know I say it too much, but she'd have been so pleased. I wish she'd have met Tucker."

"I knew she was with me that day we got married, Dad. I heard her talk to me. I really did."

Steve went back to working his hoe. Brandy knew she'd triggered a tear or two and realized he didn't want to show it.

"Where exactly did you two get these again?" he asked, pointing to the palm trees.

"It was from their last mission. They rescued a young aid worker, who'd been kidnapped and trafficked in Nigeria. Her father lives in the Portland area and sent these as a thank you."

"They're beautiful trees. You know they get tall, don't you? And they're not cheap."

"Oh yes. Tucker said he wanted to put them here in front like sentries, a good omen, protecting our family home."

"With your addition and all these gardens, you're building quite an oasis. Kind of reminds me of some of the places your mom and I visited in Italy or Southern France."

"I'd like to travel someday, see all those places. Tucker's been all over the world."

"Well, when he finishes his years with the Navy, he should have a nice retirement. Then you can travel."

"My thought exactly. Nine more years. Unless he decides to stay in longer."

Steven stopped his hoeing again. "You think he will?"

"I don't know. Now that we have Kimberly, I want him home more. But that decision is his to make and mine to support. That's how it goes on the Teams."

JOE STOPPED BY to check on the irrigation in the back yard. He'd heard the team was coming home.

"Do you know what day?"

"Shannon's expecting T.J. tomorrow."

"O-M-G. Are they back in the states?" Brandy had forgotten to check her cell phone when she woke up.

"I think so."

Brandy searched for her phone and finally found it tucked into Kimberly's diaper bag. The instant she plugged it into the charger, the messages lit up. There had been three from Tucker. "Oh crap."

She dialed and it went straight to voicemail. "I'm so sorry, Tucker. I just found out you guys will be home tomorrow. So excited here. Stuck my phone last night into Kimberly's bag and forgot all about it. Can't wait to see you! Let me know what time, and we'll be there."

Brandy did more laundry, mostly the baby's, and while Kimberly was sleeping, she washed her hair. She changed the sheets on the bed, using the freshly laundered cotton ones with the expensive softener. She prepared a special meal plan for the whole day, so she'd be ready no matter when he came home and made Tucker's favorite peanut butter brownies. Then she added a bottle of champagne to chill and checked on the beer bottle inventory, deciding it was adequate.

Now all she needed was Tucker.

Just after noon, she got the call she'd been waiting for.

"We're all done in Virginia, got a flight home tomorrow," he said. "Miss me?"

"Such a silly question! I've thought of nothing else these past couple of days."

"How about Kimberly?"

"You know how that goes. As long as she's fed and clean, she's happy. But I think she's waiting to be held by her big, strong daddy."

"You want me to bring anything back for you?"

"Nope. Just you. What time do I meet the plane?"

"We got the red-eye, leaving like 0100, so nine or ten we're estimating. Unless we get delayed."

"Perfect. We'll be there."

BRANDY HAD CALLS from several other of the wives, making sure she knew about the men getting home. It was agreed that there would be a beach get together with the kids on Friday night. She called Christy and asked her if Kyle was back in town.

"Oh, he'll be there. He doesn't like missing rotations, but it was important training."

She put the phone down to monitor kids she was babysitting. "Sorry. I'm sorry I didn't get over there to visit, Brandy. It will be great to see the baby."

"She'll be snuggled up."

"I heard you had some help from your dad."

"Yes, and Joe Benson came over and built our backyard fencing. He also built this beautiful pink playhouse, too. You'll have to bring the kids over to play in it."

"Yup, we'll plan that too. So how did Tucker do? Did he say?"

"You know Tucker. I'm afraid he had to spend more time calming me down than being able to share much of what it was like over there, but he did fine, I guess."

"So you were okay, then?"

Brandy realized too late that she'd perhaps alluded to the problems Geri and Bryce had had with their oldest. She didn't feel comfortable going there. She hadn't mentioned it to anyone but Tucker. Not even her father.

"Well, this being the first time I was alone with the baby got tough a couple of days, but I called in my chips. He told me to surround myself with the other wives and family. My fault for not thinking of that first. No worries."

"Okay, but you know you can call me if anything comes up, right? Anything."

Brandy felt slightly guilty not being completely forthcoming but didn't want to burden her.

THEN SHE GOT a call from Geri. The family was going through counseling. Lynn had gotten behind in school, but Brandy was happy to hear there had been no further contact with the creep who'd made the text messages.

"I guess your guy will be coming home any day now, so just wanted to say thanks for the support."

"Any time, Geri. I'm relieved to know things have begun to return to normal for you guys. It could have been much worse."

"You're right about that. Bryce and I talk about that all the time. You know, they had a bomb scare last year in the high school. The administration has to deal with so many issues these days, it seems."

"A bomb scare? I didn't know about that."

"Nothing was found. They evacuated the school. All a big hoax. Bryce's friend said they suspected a student, but the police couldn't prove anything."

"You don't think the two are related?"

"No. That's a completely separate thing. It was probably someone who was trying to get out of taking a test. I sure wouldn't want to be a high school principal these days."

"And here we thought our guys had the dangerous jobs."

"Well, they still do. But, honestly, all this social media stuff, like they said in the program the task force put on at St. Alma's, it's getting out of hand. Hard to protect our kids."

Worry dampened Brandy's good mood.

"We have to teach them, Brandy. I'm talking to other parents. Bryce and I felt like we really dropped the ball. We should have clamped down on her texting a long time ago. You never think anything about it, figure it's just kid stuff, but then something like what happened to Lynn occurs. They all want to be liked. They get pressured, I think."

"You're right, Geri. I see these kids dressing the way they do. Of course, I would look horrible putting on those tight shorts and tops they wear, you know. But I look at some of these girls, and they just look embarrassed to be wearing those clothes. Why do kids feel they have to do that?"

"I don't know, but you're right. And Lynn is mortified at how easy she fell for the attention. The counselor explained it was natural to feel that way and to understand she had no experience to know any better. It wasn't her fault. That it was the predator who found her, not the other way around."

Brandy made a mental note for the future. Although tragic, she was glad she was now fully aware of what could happen. She asked a question that had been worrying her. "Geri, where did those photos come from? I never heard about that?"

"They were left in her locker. He slipped them under the door."

So that meant the guy had come onto campus. It

wasn't random, after all. She shuddered and vowed to discuss it with Tucker.

"How's Keira?" she asked, trying to keep it light.

"She hasn't stopped talking about that pink play-house. I've got a call in to Joe."

"That would be nice for her."

"Well, enjoy your homecoming. I just wanted to thank you for having the guts to give us a heads-up on all of this. Without your call, it could have gotten much worse."

"You're welcome. I hope someone would do the same if it were reversed."

"When you guys want to, we'd like to take the two of you out to dinner. Until then, have fun!"

The two ladies giggled and hung up.

KIMBERLY HAD A fussy night and didn't go back to sleep, so Brandy wound up bringing her to bed with her, hoping she wouldn't now expect this new routine. As the bright sun crept into the cervices of her blackout shades, she awoke and felt she'd hardly slept at all. Of course, Kimberly was out cold. And she'd wet the bed.

Brandy decided to let her sleep until the last minute then bathed and fed her. She put the sheets in the washer and put the old ones on. So much for a lovely, scented homecoming.

At the base, she drove Tucker's Hummer, lining it

up next to all the other wives. Kimberly was the magnet of attention until they all heard the drone of the lumbering transport plane.

Her heart raced every time she heard the darned thing. The ground shook. Her stomach churned in knots. Kimberly must have heard it as well, because her expression was puzzled. With her pink rabbit ears cap, her ears were protected from most the outside noise, but Brandy knew she could still feel the rumble of the big plane until just before the thing landed and began to taxi closer to their hangar.

As the men filed out, wives and children were clutching the chain link fence for that first glimpse of their husband or father, brother or son. Unlike the time before, there wasn't a flag-draped coffin returning with the group to greet a grieving mother.

Danny and a couple other guys ran toward the gate, greeting the kids first and then wrapping their arms around the whole family. Most took their time. Brandy saw one member with a swollen eye looking very nasty. One of the women whispered, "Oh my God." The lanky SEAL shrugged and hung his head down as he approached his wife and three school-age children.

At last she noticed Tucker's swagger, that distinctive way a large man moved. Brawley had called him the steamroller SEAL. He cracked a wide smile, giving just a hint of a wave, and threaded his way through the narrow opening jammed with reuniting families. Brandy held back so she could behold him sauntering toward her.

"Well, hello there," he said, staring down at her mouth and giving her that signal he was completely hers.

She kissed him hard, careful not to squeeze Kimberly too tightly between them. He stepped back and looked the two of them up and then down again.

"Am I lucky, or am I lucky?" he said with his hands on his hips.

"You're definitely gonna get lucky."

That earned her another quick kiss, and then he pulled Kimberly from her mother's arms. "Look at you, little pink bunny princess. I'll bet you're gonna steal hearts away from tough men, just like your mamma does."

Kimberly drooled, and Brandy thought she was trying hard to focus. He nuzzled her with his nose, and kissed her cheeks, making her pull her fingers up against her face. And then she sneezed.

"It's the stubble," he whispered. "I'm not as soft and delicious as your mamma."

He handed her back. Searching behind him, nodding to men and wives here and there, he hoisted his duty bag over his shoulder.

"Let's get the hell outta here."

CHAPTER 23

THE HOUSE TUCKER had left behind was not the same house he came back to. With the garden laying out the thick, ruffled carpeting of mature vegetable plants in neat rows, the painted fencing that accentuated the border with the driveway and the two palms waving their welcome back, the transformation was astonishing.

Over the old wood floors, she had thrown bright red and brown area rugs, filled in the sparse living room furniture with an antique rocking chair and added a hand-stenciled storage chest. She had truly made their house a home.

"I can't believe what you've done," he whispered. The house was still uncluttered but fresh-looking and modern.

Brandy beamed over her shoulder, bouncing Kimberly in front against her chest. "Look at the back yard."

The pink playhouse was featured in the middle of the yard, just past the concrete patio. Redwood fencing with a lattice top design completely enclosed the space. She'd picked up a used outdoor table and chairs and had started adding plants around the perimeter.

Tucker opened the sliding glass door and walked out to examine Joe's handiwork, moving the door and window shutters back and forth on hinges. The swept and clean wooden floor made a heavenly place for his little girl to spend hours and hours of free play. Joe had even stenciled Kimberly's name over the doorway in red.

"You can't see it now, but they put a gate in on the side, so now we don't have to carry stuff through the house."

"Magnificent, honey. What a transformation. You guys were busy."

Brandy leaned against him, and he wrapped his arm around her waist. Then he began to worry.

"H-How much did all this cost?" he asked.

"Well, Dad paid for all the material, and Joe and two of his friends did the construction. Jillian gave me several things she didn't need anymore, like the furniture in the living room, an old dresser I repainted and a set of side tables you'll see in the master. So nothing, really."

"Nothing?"

"Well, I did buy some bigger clothes for Kimberly. I kind of splurged on that, but all this was done without costing us a penny."

"This is too good to be true. I'm amazed. I hadn't realized the rear fencing would make such a difference."

"I thought we could either put in bricks or do a lawn, if it wouldn't be too much work. Maybe some fruit trees?"

"Anything you want, sweetheart. Might have to wait a month or two, but I think a lawn would be nice."

Brandy led him back inside. On the dining table were a set of plans rolled up. "Here's the surprise I was talking about." She rolled out the paper, securing it from curling back with the salt and pepper shaker and a couple of magazines. "Joe has a friend who was a Civil and Structural Engineer, and he drew these up. Dad paid for the permit fees, and we turned everything in to the City for approval. Even if they approve them, we don't have to pull the permit until we're ready. In the meantime, we can still make changes. If you don't like any of it, we'll wait until we get something you do like."

His hand smoothed over the bright white surface, noting the design of a front door trellis.

"Roses, Tucker. I'd like white roses there covering the whole trellis."

The side stairway to the second floor had an observation deck. He looked over the drawings for the conversion of the downstairs stairwell into a second bath and storage.

"We need another bathroom. We have no closets!" she explained.

The engineer had also drawn ideas for adding more cabinets and countertop space in the kitchen and an addition of a flat-roofed garage on the right side of the walkway. The garage managed to hide the bottom stairs leading to up top and created a small, private yard around the back, as well as a lower floor deck area for the upper unit.

"He's thought of everything, Brandy. Don't know how we'll pay for it, but it really transforms the use of the property." Tucker hadn't seen any of this in his mind.

"Dad's been very up front about helping to pay for all this."

"But he already helped with the down payment."

"And he loves being part of this project, Tucker. Both him and Joe are excited about it, maybe even more so than I am."

His duty bag was still hung over his shoulder, and now he felt the weight of it and dropped it to the ground. It finally dawned on him that he was *home*. She was making this their home.

That this is our house.

It was time to forget all the chaos in the rest of the world and just enjoy this lovely new space with his family.

"I'm amazed. You guys were busy," he said as he wrapped his arms around her and the baby. The softness of her lips kickstarted his libido and, like an lumbering and rusty machine, began revving up and coming back to life. All the familiar smells and tastes of her wet kiss flooded his senses.

He was finally home.

HE'D STRIPPED OFF his traveling clothes and jumped into the steaming shower she'd prepared for him. As he dried off, Brandy put the baby down and waited for him on the edge of the bed. She hadn't bothered putting on anything to cover herself up. She knew it was going to stay on her body for mere seconds.

The look of her regal form, the way she held her head, waiting for him, her deep breathing, showing all the signs of her arousal, and her understanding they were back together again, and that she wanted it to be special.

He'd make sure it was special. That's what he fully intended to do. He'd thought about not much else all the way home, even as he was joking, signing reports and debriefing staff, he thought of her sitting here, for him. Waiting to bring him back to life again. This was what he was really here for, not that other stuff.

This was man's work, real man's work. His job was to make her feel more loved than she ever had in her whole life.

He approached his queen, sat and looked into her eyes, their bodies barely touching.

"Every time I think I know what it feels like to come back to you, the real thing just kicks that memory to the curb."

"Me too. But I still love the dreams," she whispered.

"Oh yes, I do too. The the real thing is better. So much better."

He started slow, kissing her neck and chest. She acted almost shy, protecting herself in her tender places with her palms as he gently kissed her, removing barriers to his touch, his tongue, to the glorious sight of her quivering body. He'd forgotten how strong she was, and also how delicate she felt beneath his hands as they lay back naked, feeling the timbre of her soul.

She arched to his touch and, as his intensity grew, she accepted him, her hands guiding and showing him she too didn't want to wait a moment longer before he could be inside her. His hand found hers, and together they explored the miracle of the space they formed as one. Then he spread her right arm first, and then the left out to the side on the bed, squeezing her fingers before releasing. He slid his fingers beneath her buttocks, raising her pelvis to accept him. His shaft entered her, drawing out that first stroke as long as he could. He watched her hitch her breath, close her eyes and then open them again with a smile. She flug her arms up, wrapping around his back with her legs around his hips so he could go deep.

She gave back all the goodness of her fierce love.

The rhythm of their bodies re-told the ancient stories men and women have shared for centuries—all about loyalty and devotion, honor and forgiveness. And the healing power of love—the most powerful emotion in the universe. That power increased the more it was shared, amplified by the constant beats of their hearts as relentless as any surf on any shore.

Brandy stayed right with him, matched his movements in her soft and gentle way, opening herself up and loving with abandon.

Her deep sigh and soft moan at their climax broke Tucker's heart, wishing the sunny morning would never end. His thumbs pressed her forehead, wiping the little beads of sweat into her hair. He devoured her hot breath and later held her like a fragile doll while she shattered beneath him.

The miracle of Brandy's body and the joining they shared filled him with gratitude. Their urgent lovemaking shed twenty years off him, washed away all the memories of where he had been and what he'd seen. The problems of that far away land subsided like memories of a movie watched years ago. He kissed her until her heart stopped racing and her breathing returned to normal. At last, he became whole and alive, healed.

Looking down on her soft face and long hair splayed over the pillows, he reveled in the magic she spun all around him. He wanted to pleasure her all over again, because he simply could never get enough.

Tucker kept vigil until she fell asleep, kissing her hair and whispering secrets she'd not remember. He loved the feel of their entwined bodies entangled in the sheets. She was his reward for coming home, and worth the price of being so far away.

In risking it all, it made having her in his arms again that much sweeter.

THE FIRST FEW days back were always dreamy after-noons and evenings filled with sex. He loved that she never denied any and all his advances, even encourag-ing him further. He demanded she not get dressed, so she took to walking around the house barefoot in her opened silk robe, bending over to pick up things she'd "accidentally" drop so he could look at her ass again. It drove him crazy, in a good way. No one would ever understand how magical those first days back would be—had to be—for him. Even working around the baby's nap times and feedings, was fun, adding a sense of urgency to their lovemaking.

He could have never imagined that life could be so perfect.

THE PLANNED TEAM beach party came three days later, starting in the afternoon and ending in a big bonfire under the stars after dark. It continued to be the tradition Kyle Lansdowne, their Team leader, had set right from the start. It was something they practiced both before and after their missions. The kids, off-spring of these men he shared his brotherhood bond with, played together as one big family.

Brawley was whole again and enjoying his instructor stint. Several others were considering retirement. Some of his brothers were getting re-married, and some were in the early throes of separation. It all added to the patchwork of their Team and the resiliency of their bond. No matter what, they would always be brothers, even if the families sometimes drifted down a different path.

Tucker knew that would never be the case with him and Brandy.

The next week he got a phone call from Bryce Tanner, asking for a meeting. They met at a local coffee shop.

"Heard you had some success over in the Canaries. Good job," said Bryce.

Tucker shrugged. "Sometimes it works out. Sometimes we come home empty-handed. Still so much more to do over there. We just do our little piece. You know."

"I do know. I know, indeed. We ship out in three days."

"South America?"

"Yup. Got some Americans stranded down there and some friends of the U.S."

"God speed."

Tucker squirmed in his seat, took another sip of his latte, and waited for Bryce to get to the point. The man was studying him, like he was going to be asked for advice. He hated giving advice to another long-time Team guy. But he'd do what he could. It was clearly not a social call.

"Tucker, I'm sure Brandy filled you in on all this stuff that happened with Lynn."

He nodded agreement and waited for Bryce's next question.

"I have a buddy on the San Diego P.D. who says they arrested a child pornographer recently—this is strictly off the record."

"I got it. Brandy said you trust him. Go on."

"Probably wouldn't surprise you to learn there are

thousands of these creeps all over the U.S. And they link hands with those that traffic in selling women and children for sex, which sometimes, if a person has means, is the next step in the chain of evil."

"Good way to put it. Happens over there as well."

"Yes, and from what I understand, over sixty percent of those children and ladies kidnapped—the ones that survive, that is—are sold to willing buyers in the U.S."

"Whoa. I didn't know that one."

"Google it. You'll see the trends."

"So this has to do with Lynn somehow? God, I pray it does not."

"Not directly, no. She fully understands what happened and that she never should have encouraged the conversation with someone she didn't know—even someone she knew who sent those texts and those disgusting pictures. Like most kids, Tucker, she knew she'd done something wrong by inviting him into our lives, and she didn't want to get in trouble, so she covered it up. I think a lot of kids behave that way."

"Understandable."

"This internet thing, the way kids are on social media—we can't protect them. We can't wait for the government to protect them. The police have their hands tied. I sometimes wonder, if we put a few SEAL teams on it, what they would do locating these rings and putting them out of business."

"In a perfect world. But we're not allowed. You know that."

"So we spread the news, wait, and hope it doesn't happen." Bryce leaned forward and drilled a look that told Tucker he was dead serious. "How well does that work overseas? Waiting, I mean?"

"That's what we're there for."

"Right. Invited by governments, provided by our government. Meanwhile, some of our kids are getting abused back at home. And do you think it will get any better on its own? I gotta hand it to the police, but they're outmatched, Tucker. You know that."

Tucker's adrenaline switch had flipped. He'd had the same thought many times over.

"What are you saying, Bryce?"

"I go over in three days. I stay perhaps two, three weeks, whatever. But when I come back, I'm thinking I'd like to do something about all this."

"How?"

Bryce checked the surrounding area to make sure he wasn't being heard. "I don't know. Perhaps find someone who could help us out? Give us an inside line on the bad guys, help support our efforts?"

"You're talking about *posse comitatus*."

"I am. Except I'm not sure it can be a government entity. Might have to be private."

"And that would be illegal, Bryce."

His friend nodded again and stared off into the distance. "I can't wait, Tucker. That's the hardest thing I could do. I'm one of the old guys now. Probably time for me to hang it up before I get injured or get someone else hurt. I need a new hip, and my knees are shot from all those jumps."

"Same here. I'll be needing new knees before I'm fifty."

"We've done good work, protecting those we love from foreign evil coming here. But we're losing the way, Tucker. It's coming anyway. We got terrorist plots and training camps, and some of us have seen them, too."

Tucker had heard the stories. It was common knowledge.

"We have to take a back seat to guys—I'm talking police and social workers—who are terrific but just don't have the same training we have. They're like janitors in our inner cities. The cleanup crew."

Bryce leaned forward again.

"We need someone to go in and take them out. As many of them as we can find."

Tucker waited before responding. "I hear what you're saying, Bryce. How are you going to know the difference? What if the wrong person gets taken out? That's why we have the courts. It's slow, and yes, some of these dudes get off, but we can't have citizens taking the law into their own hands, Bryce."

"*Most* citizens. Tell me, Tucker. Would you be able to tell the difference? If you got right up into the face of pure evil? You've seen them before, as have I. If you had the opportunity to make sure one of these creeps would never hurt another innocent child or woman, if you could bring them in to face justice, what would you do?"

It was the same thing they did overseas all the time. They weren't assassination squads, yet, things were done. Some enemies would fight to the death.

Tucker thought about the offer Colin Riley had made. He personally wasn't in a place where he could consider going to work for the man. Not yet.

But maybe he could make an introduction.

CHAPTER 24

Three months later....

TUCKER AND BRYCE flew into Portland where a black town car waited for them. The two had not spoken much since Bryce's return from his mission. Tucker had hoped Bryce had reconsidered the ideas he'd shared. But that wasn't the case. He was even more determined than before.

Bryce told him his San Diego P.D. buddy let him know that they'd solved a bomb threat case at Lynn's school last year. It had been arranged through a chat on a gaming site. A sophomore at the school paid an anonymous person five hundred dollars to hack in and email the threat to the school administration.

The student was questioned extensively, but the money transaction happened outside the banking system with crypto currency and therefore was un-traceable. It was a case of a kid who wanted a few days off from school to visit his girlfriend in the Bay Area.

The girlfriend casually mentioned it to her parents months later, and they called the police. Otherwise, no one ever would have known.

Just knowing this type of thing could happen set off red flags in Bryce. He felt more compelled than ever to somehow make a difference, make himself the barrier between evil and innocents.

Though the story wasn't about sex work or human trafficking, it very easily could have been.

Tucker told his buddy about Mr. Riley and agreed to accompany him to meet the gentleman. He wasn't going to join up, just make the introductions.

"Did he say his daughter is recovering?" Bryce asked.

"I didn't ask about her, and he didn't bring it up. Sven keeps in loose touch with her."

"You trust the man?"

"That's going to be up to you, Bryce. It's an awfully big step, doing this. I presume you've said nothing to Geri."

"Nope. We're just fishin'."

"You gotta think very hard before you jump into this. You could be sent to prison if caught. What would Geri and the kids do without you?"

"We gotta talk first. Hell, he might not like me. He might only want you," said Bryce.

"Well, he's not getting me. I'm not ready to take

that leap, and don't pressure me. It won't work. I'm doing this for you because I don't want you mixed up in something that's underfunded. This guy has billions. That part is real. The rest is up to you."

Colin Riley sat in his specialized wheelchair in the middle of his wood-paneled office overlooking the Columbia River. He briefly scanned Bryce but moved his chair forward to shake Tucker's hand first and then turned his attention to Bryce, as Tucker introduced him.

"Nice to hear from you, Tucker. Someone sent me a picture of the palm trees in your front yard. I like what you've done with the place."

Of course Riley would have done this. He'd be checking up on Tucker for the rest of his life.

"So you probably know about my daughter, then."

"I heard about that too. I think we have a little to-ken for you, something you can stash away for her college fund."

"I didn't come here for money, sir. I'm just here to make an introduction." Irritation made a familiar appearance in Tucker's gut.

"I do understand." Riley angled his head, pointing to the large leather couch placed beneath an enormous photograph of a bald eagle hanging on the wall above. "Please be seated." Mr. Riley asked Tucker to begin.

"Sir, I told Bryce some of what we discussed in the

hospital some months back. I told you then I wasn't interested, but Bryce here is."

Riley studied Tucker for several long seconds then turned his gaze to Bryce. "And what were you told Mr. Tanner?"

"You asked Tucker if he ever wanted to do something else, take care of bad guys here at home, that you might be interested in supporting him."

"Not supporting him, Bryce. May I call you that?"

"Yes, sir. You may."

"I said I'd make him rich beyond his wildest dreams."

Bryce leaned back into the back of the couch and exhaled. "Okay. Wow." Then he placed his elbows on his thighs, coming closer to the billionaire. "Tucker isn't interested. But I am."

"Your reason?"

"My daughter was recently targeted by a predator. Everyone knows the facts. The police, the FBI, everyone agrees that it would be nearly impossible to find this creep. He'll probably get caught in some raid at some future date. Or not. But day after day, there are these rings of people who traffic young girls, women. And there are thousands of them. The number is growing, not getting smaller. Tucker and I both have seen some of these human smuggling rings in action— like the one who nabbed your daughter."

"And you would consider what I asked Tucker to do?"

"I'd have to think about it. But that's what I came here to talk to you about."

Riley's eyes sparkled as he turned to Tucker. "Why did you come? Were you curious?"

"I wanted to help him, as a brother, not make a wrong decision. I don't want to see him going to jail, even if he's trying to do good here. What we're talking about is not legal. Not sanctioned by any government entity."

"Do you know others who you might be able to recruit, to set up a team, Mr. Tanner?"

"I think I do."

"Former SEALs?"

"SEALs, law enforcement, and patriots who just don't want to wait around to let someone else clean up the trash. I know men who have the skills and knowhow to make a difference."

"Like Robin Hood and his merry band, eh?" Riley chuckled.

Tucker dug his fingers into the soft leather and nearly punched four holes in it.

"With all due respect—" he began.

"I meant no insult. I meant it in the most respectful of ways. If I was healthy, it's what I'd do. I have the money, and I have the connections. But I cannot be the weapon. That part of my life is over. I don't know how much longer I have—even a simple cold is life-threatening for me. But I don't want to wither away in a rest home when I can make a difference. I want to spend my money creating good, stamping out evil, and supporting those warriors who can help me accomplish that."

Riley's eyes were unwavering. Tucker knew the man meant every word he'd just uttered. A part of him wanted to seize the chalice and grab the golden sword to take on the challenge. But the loyal husband and father and decorated Navy SEAL wasn't there yet and would not be taking that step.

"What would it take for you to join him, Tucker?" Riley pondered.

It was not a difficult decision. It wasn't even his decision to make. There was only one answer to that question.

"Time. *Lots* of time, sir."

THAT AFTERNOON RILEY and Bryce Tanner agreed to have several meetings to iron out the details before anything would be said to anyone else, including his wife. Tucker was sworn to secrecy.

On the flight home, Tucker admitted, "You're either a crazier man or a braver man than I am, Bryce. Part of me wants to go do this with you. But I just can't yet."

Bryce was thoughtful. "I'm not going to lie. I feel as excited as the day I was told I had a chance to go to BUD/S. Maybe you're the braver man, Tucker. Only time will tell."

"Roger that, my friend. You make sure you look at everything before you commit. And I'm going to have to work on my conscience if anything happens to you. But damn, wouldn't it be great if it would work?"

"And then you can join me."

"Not promising. Don't say that." He chuckled. "Now you have to come up with some awesome name like *Posse International*."

"*Fuck You Society.*"

"*Elimination Inc.*"

"I got a better one. How about Bone Frog Protection?"

Tucker smiled to himself.

Yeah, that would work.

CHAPTER 25

B RANDY HAD TRIED for days to find out about his
fishing trip with Bryce. Tucker came back from it
like he'd just spent two weeks at a Man Camp or
Olympic Training Camp, she told him. He was light on
his feet, happy, and fully engaged in life. It was as
though he'd finally had an epiphany and had settled
into his own skin.

She watched him closer that day, Tucker holding
Kimberly on his belly, her arms and legs moving as he
played horseshoes with Bryce, who was now a frequent
visitor. Bryce was like one of the Team 3 guys.

Geri had told her that Tucker had given Bryce
some really good advice. When she asked about it, Geri
said she had no idea, just that they'd had a long talk
and both of them got clear about what their life's
purpose was going forward.

He knew he was going to have to tell her something. She wouldn't let up. She'd gotten a bead on this

thing between he and Bryce, and she wouldn't let go.

Re-enlistments, if it happened when they were overseas, netted them extra bonuses at signing. But when that opportunity came and went, Bryce had made the decision not to renew his hitch and started his disassociation paperwork. A small ripple had been caused in the community, wondering what he was going to do.

Tucker didn't care about it. He actually felt settled, good about his decision to watch Bryce do something he wanted to do. Tucker wasn't there yet, and he'd been honest with Riley, and with his Team buddy.

"There's one thing I've been wondering about, Tucker," she said as he stepped out of the shower.

Here it comes. She was asking very sweetly, so naked and rubbing herself all over him. It was a twisted way of getting information out of him, but Hell, he was game for making love to his stubborn wife however she got to that point.

"What's that?" He was looking at her standing behind him in the mirror.

She began to dry off his back, kissed him in several places along his spine, at the same time letting him feel the bare skin of her thighs rubbing against the backs of his. She pressed her breasts into his back, allowed the towel to travel from his chest, down his hip, and then drop. She squeezed him which was one of his favorite things. He flipped around to face her.

"What is it, Brandy?" He begged her to tease him, say something either dirty or inappropriate.

"What happened on that fishing trip?"

His quick intake of air almost let the cat out of the bag. He didn't want to reveal their conversation, or decision.

She gave him a wicked smile. "Should I be jealous?"

"Hell no." He abruptly moved away, grabbed a glass, and poured himself a drink of water. "Why do you ask?"

"You've just had this cat-that-ate-the-canary look to you ever since. And now Bryce is leaving the teams. Are you thinking about doing that too?"

"Why would I do that?" He knew she was beginning to suspect something. She'd pushed too far, and now he was getting annoyed.

"Come here, Brandy. Let's talk."

He took her by the hand, bringing her into the bedroom, sat down, and had her sit on his bare legs. Her silk shortie robe opened down the front. He licked his lips as he focused on the way her nipples knotted between his thumb and fingers.

"I love everything about you, Brandy. Some days, when I see you lying asleep or watch you nursing Kimberly, I think to myself that perhaps I don't deserve this."

"Nonsense," she said, moving against him, pushing him back on the bed, placing her knees on either sides of his hips and delicately riding him, teasing to get him snagged. He tried to angle his hips to facilitate this.

"You're silly," she whispered, watching him play with her.

"I mean it," he said, his fingers now squeezing her tits.

She rose up and then deliciously settled back down on him, touching and squeezing the base of his shaft as he plunged in slowly. She leaned forward, tilting her rear up. He bent his knees, forced his hips upward, thrusting so deep she caught her breath. Her internal muscles took hold and she leaned back and sighed.

"Oh God, Tucker. I never want this to end. I want us to fuck like this forever."

The conversation was gone. The only thing he could focus on was making Brandy explode. He stepped up his pace, grabbing her hips, grinding them down on him, then rose her up so he could pump in and out until his speed caused her to scream, "Yes!"

"Absolutely, sweetheart. You want more?'

"Always."

"Always what?"

"Always more." She was going to object as he kept up his furious pace, but she corrected him. "Always fuck me more."

"That's my girl." He could feel she was going to come again for the second time. He was having a hard time holding back.

"Tucker?"

"Yes, Brandy?" He was losing it. He felt her muscles in that delicious spasm of hers. She forced herself harder against him with each stroke.

"I want to fuck all night long. Can we please—"

Finally! She'd lost her train of thought. He started to spill.

"Would you fuck me all night long?"

"If I'm physically able, you bet."

"And Tucker?" He was coming inside her, his hot sperm coating her everywhere.

"No more questions, Brandy. Sweetheart, I just want to do this."

God, she was stubborn!

BUT OF COURSE, Brandy never forgot a thing. As soon has he'd nearly passed out, she was at it again.

"That happiness in you. Tell me what it is," she asked.

Her body was still sweaty. He knew he wouldn't have much more time until she'd have to get up and feed the baby again.

He drew his arm up over his forehead, thinking all while his shaft was growing again.

"Bryce has decided to follow a different path, one that I cannot take. At least not yet."

"Go on."

"That's it, really. You are more precious to me than my own life. I've got everything I need here."

"And Bryce?"

"He's going to chase some demons. He wants revenge. He wants to balance the scales of good and evil. All I want to do is complete my job and come home to you, Brandy. I would never do anything to get in the way of that."

She would tell him later that his kisses were sweeter that night. He'd walked through some kind of a threshold recently and it didn't really have anything to do with her. He didn't have the demons Bryce did.

He'd told her that he thought she was stronger than he was. She told him he was so wrong. That he'd taught her how to love him.

And it was the easiest thing in the world to do.

He vowed he'd keep teaching her, because without her, his life would become hard and small. He wanted the pink miracle that was their family.

He didn't care who thought that was funny. It was the damned truth!

Have you enjoyed Brandy and Tucker's story? Stay tuned for more episodes, including some of the other men who might find themselves part of the Bone Frog

Protection team. One by one, they'll decide where their higher calling comes from. They'll rise to the challenge.

If you are new to my books, you might want to start with the very first SEAL Brotherhood book, **Accidental SEAL**. Or, with the **Ultimate SEAL Collection**, which has the first four books in the series, with two bonus novellas.

Or, you can read any of the other popular series:
Bad Boys of SEAL Team 3
Band of Bachelors

And if you haven't read the other Bone Frog books, Check out Books 1-4 here.

ABOUT THE AUTHOR

 NYT and USA Today best-selling author Sharon Hamilton's award-winning Navy SEAL Brotherhood series have been a fan favorite from the day the first one was released. They've earned her the coveted Amazon author ranking of #1 in Romantic Suspense, Military Romance and Contemporary Romance categories, as well as in Gothic Romance for her Vampires of Tuscany and Guardian Angels. Her characters follow a sometimes rocky road to redemption through passion and true love.

Now that he's out of the Navy, Sharon can share with her readers that her son spent a decade as a Navy SEAL, and he's the inspiration for her books.

Her Golden Vampires of Tuscany are not like any vamps you've read about before, since they don't go to ground and can walk around in the full light of the sun.

Her Guardian Angels struggle with the human charges they are sent to save, often escaping their vanilla world of Heaven for the brief human one. You won't find any of these beings in any Sunday school class.

She lives in Sonoma County, California with her husband and her Doberman, Tucker. A lifelong organic gardener, when she's not writing, she's getting *verra verra* dirty in the mud, or wandering Farmers Markets looking for new Heirloom varieties of vegetables and flowers. She and her husband plan to cure their wanderlust (or make it worse) by traveling in their Diesel Class A Pusher, Romance Rider. Starting with this book, all her writing will be done on the road.

She loves hearing from her fans:
Sharonhamilton2001@gmail.com

Her website is:
sharonhamiltonauthor.com

Find out more about Sharon, her upcoming releases, appearances and news from her newsletter, **AND receive a free book** when you sign up for Sharon's newsletter.

Facebook:
facebook.com/SharonHamiltonAuthor

Twitter:
twitter.com/sharonlhamilton

Pinterest:
pinterest.com/AuthorSharonH

Amazon:
amazon.com/Sharon-Hamilton/e/B004FQQMAC

BookBub:
bookbub.com/authors/sharon-hamilton

Youtube:

youtube.com/channel/UCDInkxXFpXp_4Vnq08ZxMBQ

Soundcloud:

soundcloud.com/sharon-hamilton-1

Sharon Hamilton's Rockin' Romance Readers:

facebook.com/groups/sealteamromance

Sharon Hamilton's Goodreads Group:

goodreads.com/group/show/199125-sharon-hamilton-readers-group

Visit Sharon's Online Store:

sharon-hamilton-author.myshopify.com

Join Sharon's Review Teams:

eBook Reviews:

sharonhamiltonassistant@gmail.com

Audio Reviews:

sharonhamiltonassistant@gmail.com

Life is one fool thing after another.
Love is two fool things after each other.

REVIEWS

"An excellent paranormal romance that was exciting, romantic, entertaining and very satisfying to read. It had me anticipating what would happen next many times over, so much so I could not put it down and even finished it up in a day. The vampires in this book were different from your average vampire, but I enjoy different variations and changes to the same old stuff. It made for a more unpredictable read and more adventurous to explore! Vampire lovers, any paranormal readers and even those who love the romance genre will enjoy Honeymoon Bite."

"This is the first non-Seal book of this author's I have read and I loved it. There is a cast-like hierarchy in this vampire community with humans at the very bottom and Golden vampires at the top. Lionel is a dark vampire who are servants of the Goldens. Phoebe is a Golden who has not decided if she will remain human or accept the turning to become a vampire. Either way she and Lionel can never be together since it is forbidden.

I enjoyed this story and I am looking forward to the next installment."

"A hauntingly romantic read. Old love lost and new love found. Family, heart, intrigue and vampires. Grabbed my attention and couldn't put down. Would definitely recommend."

PRAISE FOR THE
SEAL BROTHERHOOD SERIES

"Fans of Navy SEAL romance, I found a new author to feed your addiction. Finely written and loaded delicious with moments, Sharon Hamilton's storytelling satisfies like a thick bar of chocolate." —Marliss Melton, bestselling author of the *Team Twelve* Navy SEALs series

"Sharon Hamilton does an EXCELLENT job of fitting all the characters into a brotherhood of SEALS that may not be real but sure makes you feel that you have entered the circle and security of their world. The stories intertwine with each book before...and each book after and THAT is what makes Sharon Hamilton's SEAL Brotherhood Series so very interesting. You won't want to put down ANY of her books and they will keep you reading into the night when you should be sleeping. Start with this book...and you will not want to stop until you've read the whole series and then...you will be waiting for Sharon to write the next one." (5 Star Review)

"Kyle and Christy explode all over the pages in this first book, *[Accidental SEAL]*, in a whole new series of SEALs. If the twist and turns don't get your heart jumping, then maybe the suspense will. This is a must read for those that are looking for love and adventure with a little sloppy love thrown in for good measure." (5 Star Review)

PRAISE FOR THE
BAD BOYS OF SEAL TEAM 3 SERIES

"I love reading this series! Once you start these books, you can hardly put them down. The mix of romance and suspense keeps you turning the pages one right after another! Can't wait until the next book!" (5 Star Review)

"I love all of Sharon's Seal books, but *[SEAL's Code]* may just be her best to date. Danny and Luci's journey is filled with a wonderful insight into the Native American life. It is a love story that will fill you with warmth and contentment. You will enjoy Danny's journey to become a SEAL and his reasons for it. Good job Sharon!" (5 Star Review)

PRAISE FOR THE
BAND OF BACHELORS SERIES

"*[Lucas]* was the first book in the Band of Bachelors series and it was a phenomenal start. I loved how we got to see the other SEALs we all love and we got a look at Lucas and Marcy. They had an instant attraction, and their love was very intense. This book had it all, suspense, steamy romance, humor, everything you want in a riveting, outstanding read. I can't wait to read the next book in this series." (5 Star Review)

PRAISE FOR THE
TRUE BLUE SEALS SERIES

"Keep the tissues box nearby as you read *True Blue SEALs: Zak* by Sharon Hamilton. I imagine more than I wish to that the circumstances surrounding Zak and Amy are all too real for returning military personnel and their families. Ms. Hamilton has put us right in the middle of struggles and successes that these two high school sweethearts endure. I have read several of Sharon Hamilton's military romances but will say this is the most emotionally intense of the ones that I have read. This is a well-written, realistic story with authentic characters that will have you rooting for them and proud of those who serve to keep us safe. This is an author who writes amazing stories that you love and cry with the characters. Fans of Jessica Scott and Marliss Melton will want to add Sharon Hamilton to their list of realistic military romance writers." (5 Star Review)

"Dear FATHER IN HEAVEN,

If I may respectfully say so sometimes you are a strange God. Though you love all mankind,

It seems you have special predilections too.

You seem to love those men who can stand up alone who face impossible odds, Who challenge every bully and every tyrant ~

Those men who know the heat and loneliness of Calvary. Possibly you cherish men of this stamp because you recognize the mark of your only son in them.

Since this unique group of men known as the SEALs know Calvary and suffering, teach them now the mystery of the resurrection ~ that they are indestructible, that they will live forever because of their deep faith in you.

And when they do come to heaven, may I respectfully warn you, Dear Father, they also know how to celebrate. So please be ready for them when they insert under your pearly gates.

Bless them, their devoted Families and their Country on this glorious occasion.

We ask this through the merits of your Son, Christ Jesus the Lord, Amen."

By Reverend E.J. McMalhon S.J. LCDR, CHC, USN
Awards Ceremony SEAL Team One
1975 At NAB, Coronado

Made in the
USA
Columbia, SC